Broken dreams . . .

In that moment, crouched on the floor of the studio, Patty knew she wasn't going to become a dancer, not in the way she wanted to be. She'd never dance Swan Lake in front of a huge crowd, or travel around the world as a ballerina. She wasn't ever going to be anything but plain old Patty Gilbert, stuck in a brace.

"Patty?" Kerry asked, looking worried. "Are you OK? Say something!" She bent over next to Patty just as a tear ran down Patty's cheek. "Oh, no—you're hurt, aren't you? It's all my fault. We shouldn't have been doing all those jumps!"

Patty shook her head, as the tears started to flow more freely. "It's not . . . your fault," she choked out. Then she got to her feet and ran out of the studio.

Bantam Books in the Sweet Valley Twins and Friends® series
Ask your bookseller for the books you have missed.

#1 BEST FRIENDS
#2 TEACHER'S PET
#3 THE HAUNTED HOUSE
#4 CHOOSING SIDES
#5 SNEAKING OUT
#6 THE NEW GIRL
#7 THREE'S A CROWD
#8 FIRST PLACE
#9 AGAINST THE RULES
#10 ONE OF THE GANG
#11 BURIED TREASURE
#12 KEEPING SECRETS
#13 STRETCHING THE TRUTH
#14 TUG OF WAR
#15 THE OLDER BOY
#16 SECOND BEST
#17 BOYS AGAINST GIRLS
#18 CENTER OF ATTENTION
#19 THE BULLY
#20 PLAYING HOOKY
#21 LEFT BEHIND
#22 OUT OF PLACE
#23 CLAIM TO FAME
#24 JUMPING TO CONCLUSIONS
#25 STANDING OUT
#26 TAKING CHARGE
#27 TEAMWORK
#28 APRIL FOOL!
#29 JESSICA AND THE BRAT ATTACK
#30 PRINCESS ELIZABETH
#31 JESSICA'S BAD IDEA
#32 JESSICA ON STAGE
#33 ELIZABETH'S NEW HERO

#34 JESSICA, THE ROCK STAR
#35 AMY'S PEN PAL
#36 MARY IS MISSING
#37 THE WAR BETWEEN THE TWINS
#38 LOIS STRIKES BACK
#39 JESSICA AND THE MONEY MIX-UP
#40 DANNY MEANS TROUBLE
#41 THE TWINS GET CAUGHT
#42 JESSICA'S SECRET
#43 ELIZABETH'S FIRST KISS
#44 AMY MOVES IN
#45 LUCY TAKES THE REINS
#46 MADEMOISELLE JESSICA
#47 JESSICA'S NEW LOOK
#48 MANDY MILLER FIGHTS BACK
#49 THE TWINS' LITTLE SISTER
#50 JESSICA AND THE SECRET STAR
#51 ELIZABETH THE IMPOSSIBLE
#52 BOOSTER BOYCOTT
#53 THE SLIME THAT ATE SWEET VALLEY
#54 THE BIG PARTY WEEKEND
#55 BROOKE AND HER ROCK-STAR MOM
#56 THE WAKEFIELDS STRIKE IT RICH
#57 BIG BROTHER'S IN LOVE!
#58 ELIZABETH AND THE ORPHANS
#59 BARNYARD BATTLE
#60 CIAO, SWEET VALLEY!
#61 JESSICA THE NERD
#62 SARAH'S DAD AND SOPHIA'S MOM
#63 POOR LILA!
#64 THE CHARM SCHOOL MYSTERY
#65 PATTY'S LAST DANCE

Sweet Valley Twins and Friends Super Editions

#1 THE CLASS TRIP
#2 HOLIDAY MISCHIEF
#3 THE BIG CAMP SECRET
#4 THE UNICORNS GO HAWAIIAN

Sweet Valley Twins and Friends Super Chiller Editions

#1 THE CHRISTMAS GHOST
#2 THE GHOST IN THE GRAVEYARD
#3 THE CARNIVAL GHOST
#4 THE GHOST IN THE BELL TOWER

Sweet Valley Twins and Friends Magna Edition

#1 THE MAGIC CHRISTMAS

SWEET VALLEY TWINS
AND FRIENDS

Patty's
Last
Dance

Written by
Jamie Suzanne

Created by
FRANCINE PASCAL

A BANTAM SKYLARK BOOK
NEW YORK · TORONTO · LONDON · SYDNEY · AUCKLAND

RL 4, 008–012

PATTY'S LAST DANCE
A Bantam Skylark Book / January 1993

*Sweet Valley High and Sweet Valley Twins and Friends are
registered trademarks of Francine Pascal*

Conceived by Francine Pascal

*Produced by Daniel Weiss Associates, Inc.
33 West 17th Street
New York, NY 10011*

Cover art by James Mathewuse

To Andrew Phillip Kriss

One

◇

"I can't believe we made it," Amy Sutton exclaimed, throwing herself into a chair in front of the television.

"With time to spare," Julie Porter said, glancing at her watch. "The show doesn't start for a couple of minutes."

Elizabeth Wakefield switched on the TV. It was Friday afternoon, and she and her friends had run all the way home from Sweet Valley Middle School to watch their favorite new show, *You'll Never Believe This!* "I'm dying of thirst. Do you guys want something to drink?" she asked.

"Sure, whatever you have," Julie said.

"Me too," Amy added.

"I'll get some juice." Elizabeth walked into the

kitchen. She had just poured three glasses of orange juice when the door opened. Her twin sister, Jessica, walked into the kitchen, followed by her friends Lila Fowler and Mandy Miller. "Hi, Lizzie," Jessica said. She grabbed one of the glasses out of Elizabeth's hand, and drank down half of the juice in one gulp. "Thanks! How did you know I'd be thirsty when I got home?"

Elizabeth rolled her eyes. "Very funny, Jess." She went to the cupboard to get another glass. "While I'm at it, do you guys want some juice, too?"

"Is that orange juice from concentrate?" Lila asked, wrinkling her nose. "You must be joking."

Elizabeth decided to take that as a "no." Lila was the richest and snobbiest girl in school. Sometimes Elizabeth didn't understand how her sister could be such good friends with Lila, but then, sometimes Elizabeth didn't understand Jessica at all. Even though Elizabeth and Jessica were identical on the outside, with their long, blond hair and blue-green eyes, they were very different on the inside.

Elizabeth enjoyed having long conversations with her close friends, going horseback riding, and working on the sixth-grade newspaper. She also liked spending time by herself, reading mystery novels or writing in her journal. She wanted to be a writer when she grew up.

Jessica, on the other hand, preferred hanging

out with her friends at the mall. She was a member of the Unicorn Club, an exclusive group of the prettiest and most popular girls at school. Elizabeth didn't know how Jessica and the other Unicorns could spend so much time gossiping about boys, makeup, and soap operas.

But one thing the twins could agree on was their new favorite show. *You'll Never Believe This!* was already incredibly popular, even though it had only been on for a few weeks. The show featured videos of people trying to break local, state, or world records.

"It's starting!" Amy called out. Elizabeth, Jessica, Mandy, and Lila rushed into the living room.

"Hello, everyone, and welcome to . . ." Hollywood Jones, the show's host, paused.

"You'll never believe this!" the television audience shouted. There was loud applause, and Hollywood Jones grinned into the camera.

"He's totally gorgeous," Mandy said. "I'd give anything to meet him."

"Oh, come on, Mandy. He must be at least thirty-five years old," Julie said.

"So? That doesn't mean he's not gorgeous." Mandy leaned forward on the couch.

As the applause died down, Hollywood winked at the camera. Elizabeth had to admit it— he *was* good looking. He had short, sandy-brown hair and piercing blue eyes. "Today we'll be watching a group in San Francisco trying to break the record for eating blueberry pancakes, and then we'll travel down to San Jose, where two six-year-old girls are going to jump rope for five hours. But before we get started, I'd like to announce that *You'll Never Believe This!* is going on the road. Starting next week, we'll be traveling all over, visiting your town to see what kinds of interesting things people are up to. Our first stop will be Sacramento, and then we'll go on to . . ." He paused and glanced at a cue card. "Sweet Valley."

"What?" Lila screeched.

"No way," Amy exclaimed.

"He's coming to Sweet Valley?" Jessica shrieked as a commercial flashed on the screen. "All right!"

"I don't believe it," Mandy said. "Hollywood Jones is coming *here.* We have to do something!"

"Definitely," Jessica said. "But what?"

"We could stand on our heads for a really long time," Julie suggested.

Jessica shook her head. "Sorry. But I'm not going to appear on national TV standing on my head."

Mandy giggled. "We could have them film one of the Hairnet's classes. She definitely breaks the world record for boredom."

Elizabeth laughed, picturing their social-studies teacher, Mrs. Arnette, lecturing on TV. "I bet the ratings would go way down after that show."

"We could take them to the school cafeteria on

a Wednesday," Amy said. "They'd never believe how bad the tacos are."

"Or we could show them how dorky the guys are in gym class," Lila said. "Today we had to learn ballroom dancing again, and I got stuck with Randy Mason. It was a nightmare. I have bruises all over my—"

"Hey—that's a great idea!" Mandy cried. "We could dance!"

"What do you mean?" Jessica asked.

"You know, dance. To music," Mandy said. "Only we'll try to do it longer than anyone else ever has."

"You mean a dance marathon?" Elizabeth asked.

Mandy nodded. "Exactly. It won't be that hard, because we'll have fun doing it."

"That's a great idea," Amy said. "We can get a lot of people to do it."

"It'll be great practice for the school dance next month," Jessica added. "Mandy, you're a genius!"

"I know, I know," Mandy said. She stood up and gave an exaggerated bow. Jessica laughed and threw a pillow at her.

"Do you really think a lot of people will want to do it?" Julie asked.

"Sure. If all the Unicorns are doing it, everyone else in school will want to be in on it too," Jessica said.

Elizabeth rolled her eyes. "Well, anyway, we should start asking people right away."

"Elizabeth's right," Mandy said. "This is big news. It can't wait until Monday."

"We can tell everybody we see at the mall tomorrow," Lila suggested. "And Jessica, don't you have your ballet class tonight?"

Jessica nodded. "I can ask everyone in my class, and in the advanced class, too. Kerry Glenn, Patty Gilbert . . ."

"Kerry will definitely do it," said Mandy. "I don't know about Patty."

"She's a great dancer. You should see her," Jessica said. "She was awesome at the ballet school's last recital. Remember, Lizzie?"

Elizabeth nodded. "I don't know how interested she'll be in the dance marathon, though. She's pretty intense. All I've ever heard her talk about is ballet."

"Hey, dancing is dancing. It doesn't hurt to ask," Jessica said. "She might do it."

Elizabeth nodded. "You're right. She does seem really nice. Maybe she's just shy."

Mandy jumped to her feet. "I'm going to go home right now and check the record for dance marathons."

"Whatever it is, we're going to break it," Jessica said. "No problem!"

*   *   *

Patty Gilbert put both hands on the barre, the wooden handrail that stretched along three sides of the room, and lowered herself into a *demi-plié*, bending her knees slightly. She enjoyed stretching by herself before her advanced ballet class began their formal exercises. Patty gently rose back up, then bent down again, this time in second position. As she did, she watched herself in the full-length mirror that circled the studio. Her light-brown skin contrasted nicely with her pale orange leotard, and thin orange barrettes held her thick shoulder-length hair off her face.

"Hi, Patty." Kerry Glenn took a place next to her at the barre and started doing her own exercises. Her long, dark-brown hair was pulled back into a tight braid and wound around in a bun. She was wearing a bright, floral-patterned leotard, white tights, and bright pink leg warmers. "How's it going?"

"OK," Patty said. She continued to stretch.

"Did you hear about the big dance at school next month?" Kerry asked.

Patty shrugged. She had heard an announcement about the first all-middle-school dance earlier that week. "I'm not really interested," she said.

"Really? I think it sounds great," Kerry said. "There's going to be a live band and everything."

Patty didn't respond. She wanted to concentrate on her placing as she started her *grands pliés*. She imagined a line running straight down her spine, and another line going across her hips. She wasn't really interested in talking with Kerry. The way she saw it, Kerry was her number-one competition.

Patty had been taking ballet class since she was seven. Now that she was finally in the advanced level at the dance studio, she wanted to be the best. Kerry, a sixth-grader, had moved up from an intermediate class just a few months earlier, but already she was competing with Patty for the lead roles in recitals. Patty was a year older, and she'd studied ballet a lot longer, but at the auditions for their *Swan Lake* performance Kerry had done almost as well as Patty. Madame Baril was supposed to announce whom she'd chosen for the lead role today, and Patty couldn't help feeling nervous.

Patty wanted to win the part more than anything. Ballet was the most important thing in the world to her. She went to Madame Baril's advanced class five afternoons a week, and on the weekends she practiced at home, and sometimes rented videos of famous ballets. She was hoping to convince her parents to let her attend ballet academy full-time when she turned fourteen.

She bent her knees, being careful not to let her heels lift off the floor. Beside her, Kerry was doing the same thing. Patty couldn't help noticing how perfectly Kerry held her position.

"All right, girls." Madame Baril clapped her hands. "I have an announcement to make."

Patty pulled up her leg warmers and headed toward the center of the studio where her teacher was standing.

"I thought she would wait until the end of class," Jo Morris whispered, walking beside Patty.

"So did I," Tina Serai said. "I'm so nervous!"

As usual, Madame Baril was not smiling. She was the toughest ballet teacher Patty had ever had —the other girls called her Madame Bear behind her back. But Patty admired her. If anyone could help Patty become a great dancer, it was Madame Baril. She had danced with famous companies all around the world before retiring to become a teacher. One of her former pupils had gone on to become a prima ballerina, and Patty hoped to follow in her footsteps.

"Now, as you know, we will be performing a scene from *Swan Lake* in three weeks," Madame said. She pulled her wraparound sweater tighter around her thin frame. "For this scene, we will need several girls in the *corps*, to act as swans. Unfortunately, there can be only one Odette, the Swan Queen."

Patty nervously scuffed her ballet shoes against the hardwood floor. She looked over at Kerry and saw that she was biting her nails.

"The role of Odette is demanding," Madame Baril continued. "Not only must you be graceful, you must be strong. This was a difficult decision for me to make. But I have decided that this year, the role of Odette will be danced by Patty Gilbert."

Patty felt a surge of excitement shoot through her body. She had done it! She had won the lead role—over Kerry and everybody!

"Congratulations, Patty." Patty looked up to see Kerry smiling at her. "I think you'll make a terrific Odette."

Patty couldn't help but smile back.

"Jana, you won't believe it," Patty cried as she ran into her sister's bedroom. Jana was standing in front of her mirror, adjusting the black belt she was wearing with her old, faded jeans and crisp white blouse.

Jana turned around. "What happened? Wait—did you—"

Patty nodded. "I did it! I'm going to be Odette!"

Jana reached out and grabbed her in a bear hug. "My sister, the star," Jana said. "I'll have to get a big gold star and put it on your bedroom door."

Patty giggled. "And you can only let really important people in to talk to me."

"Right, like Mikhail Baryshnikov," Jana said. "If he's lucky."

"Well, I wouldn't go *that* far." Patty let go of Jana's hands. "First I have to make my big debut in Sweet Valley. I hope I don't mess up."

Jana picked up some silver hoop earrings from her dresser. "Patty, don't even try to tell me you're nervous, because I know you're not. You don't *get* nervous." She put the earrings in and picked up a tube of lip gloss.

"Yeah," Patty said, smiling. "You're right. I'm not nervous. I wish we could start rehearsing tonight!"

Just then there was the sound of a car honking outside. Jana pulled her curtains aside and looked out the window. "There's Dana, Robert, and Mike. I have to go." She grabbed a black leather jacket from the back of her chair and threw it over her shoulder. "I left a note for Mom and Dad on the fridge to remind them that I won't be here for dinner. We're eating at the Dairi Burger, then going to a movie."

"Sounds like fun," Patty said.

"Congratulations again," Jana called on her way down the hall. "I can't wait for opening night!"

A few seconds later, Patty heard the front door slam. She went over to the window and watched her sister get into the car with her friends.

She walked down the stairs of the quiet house, wishing she had someone to celebrate with.

Two

◇

"I'm so glad Mr. Clark's going to let us use the gym for the dance marathon," Jessica said. It was Monday, and she and Lila were walking down the hall toward the lunchroom. "And my dad offered to come and be the official timekeeper. This whole thing is coming together so fast. I—hold on a second." She had just spotted Bruce Patman walking down the hall in front of them.

"You're not going to ask *him*, are you?" Lila said. Bruce, a seventh-grader, was very handsome and very rich. He could also be a real jerk when he wanted to be.

All of the Unicorns considered Bruce one of the most important, popular guys in the seventh grade. Jessica had always thought that he was cute. But she was already sort of going out with Aaron Dallas, another sixth-grader. "Sure I'm going to ask him," Jessica whispered. "If he says he'll do it, so will practically every guy in school. Not to mention all the girls."

Jessica picked up her pace and caught up with Bruce just as he was walking into the lunchroom. To her surprise, he was the one who spoke first.

"Hey, Jessica," he said, casually leaning against the wall. "What's up?"

Jessica felt a little flustered. "Oh, uh, we're organizing a dance marathon. We're going to try to get on *You'll Never Believe This!*"

"Really?" Bruce looked impressed. "Is there anything I can do to help?"

Jessica couldn't remember the last time Bruce had been so nice to her. Usually he either ignored her or teased her. "Actually, if you could get your friends to be in it, that would be great. We want as many people as we can get."

Bruce nodded. "No problem. I'll be there." He turned and glanced over at a table of his buddies. "Hey, Jessica, you'll save a dance for me, won't you?" Then he smiled at her and walked off to join his friends.

Lila had been listening to the whole conversation. "Wow," she said, looking jealous. "Bruce Patman wants to dance with *you*?"

Jessica smiled. "What can I say?"

"Maybe he's delirious with hunger," Lila said,

as they walked over to the Unicorner, the table where the Unicorns met every day for lunch.

"I don't think so," Jessica said haughtily. "I'm sure he's just finally recognized my true charms."

"Hey, we just saw you talking to Bruce," Belinda Layton said as Jessica sat down.

"I was just asking him to help with the marathon," Jessica said casually, pulling a sandwich out of her bag.

"And he was just asking *her* to dance with him," Lila informed the group.

"You're kidding," Janet Howell said.

"What did you say?" Tamara Chase asked.

"I said I would, of course," Jessica said.

"What about Aaron?" Mandy asked.

"It's a marathon. We all have to dance with everybody if we want to break the record. Aaron and I don't have to dance together for every song," Jessica said.

Just then she spotted her twin walking into the lunchroom. She was surprised to see Elizabeth heading right for the Unicorns' table. She usually ate with her own friends.

"Hi," Elizabeth said, walking up to the table. "I was just at the library, and I found out some bad news."

"We're having another library tour?" Mary Wallace joked.

"We'd better not be," Ellen Riteman said. "I

fell asleep during the last one and I got a detention."

"No, it's not that. I was looking up the records for dance marathons," Elizabeth explained.

"Great!" Mandy said. "I searched our house all weekend, but I couldn't find the book with the world records in it. I think my little brother, Archie, must have eaten it."

"Well, guess what," Elizabeth said. "If we want to break the world record, we have to start today and dance for the next seven months."

Jessica dropped her sandwich. "What?"

Elizabeth nodded. "And if we want to break the state record, we have to dance for four weeks."

"We can't do that," Ellen said. "For one thing, they wouldn't let us skip school."

"I did find one category that I think we could shoot for," Elizabeth said. "There's an under-fourteen category in California that we could try to break."

"Under fourteen?" Janet sank down in her chair. "How humiliating."

"So, what's that record? A couple of hours or something?" Kimberly Haver asked.

Elizabeth shook her head. "It's eleven hours and thirteen minutes."

"Eleven hours and thirteen minutes?" Jessica repeated. She couldn't believe it. She was going to have to dance with Bruce a hundred times if she wanted to last that long!

"So we have to aim for twelve hours if we want to break it," Belinda said.

"Are you kidding?" Janet said. "Forget twelve hours. We have to dance for eleven hours, thirteen minutes, and two seconds."

"I'd say eleven hours, thirteen minutes, and *one* second," Ellen put in.

"Maybe we should try another record," Kimberly suggested. "Couldn't you guys think of anything else?"

"Look, we said we'd do this. We can't back out of it now," Mandy said. "Anyway, eleven hours isn't that long. We'll just have to get a really good DJ and keep things exciting."

Jessica wasn't so sure. From the looks on everyone's faces, it was going to take more than a good disc jockey. It was going to take a miracle.

The first thing Patty did when she got to the dance studio on Monday afternoon was to walk around the auditorium where all of the performances were given. She walked across the stage, trying to get a feel for it. She looked out at the rows of empty seats, picturing how she would feel when they were full of people. She couldn't wait.

She went into the changing room and put on her tights and leotard. As she tied the ribbons of her shoes around her ankles, Kerry sat down on the bench beside her and started untying her tennis shoes. "Hi, Patty," she said cheerfully.

"Hi," Patty said. She didn't look up. She was intent on getting her ribbons tied just right.

"How was your weekend?" Kerry asked.

"OK." Patty stood up and started to pin back her hair.

A few of the other girls filed into the changing room, and Patty took the opportunity to escape from Kerry into the studio. It wasn't that she didn't like Kerry. She just didn't want to be friends with her, not when they were going to be competing for the same roles. Besides, friends got in the way of ballet.

She was leaning over the box of rosin in the corner, rubbing some onto the bottoms of her shoes, when Madame Baril walked up behind her, startling her. "Patty, would you stand up straight for me, please?" she said.

Patty quickly rubbed in the last bit of the sticky rosin and stood up straight. Madame Baril walked in a circle around her, a slight frown on her face.

Patty made sure she was standing correctly, stomach tucked in, shoulders down, chin lifted, toes pointed out. "Are you judging my size for my costume?" she asked.

"No, no. A seamstress will do that later. I just thought I saw—well, never mind. It's nothing," Madame Baril said.

Standing at the barre a few minutes later, Patty concentrated extra hard on her *pliés*, making sure her lines were perfectly straight. Out of the corner of her eye, she saw Madame watching her even more closely than usual. At one point, Madame came over and stood directly behind Patty, watching her go up and down in a series of *battements glissades*. She gently put her hands on Patty's hips. "Let me see you do that again."

Patty felt a hot blush on her cheeks as she slid her right foot into second position. She lifted her foot off the ground, keeping her toes pointed, then lowered it, and slid her foot back into first position.

"Hm," Madame said. She let go of Patty's hips. "Something seems a bit off to me today, but it is probably nothing. Continue." She walked away and started watching the other girls.

Patty tried as hard as she could to make every one of her remaining warm-up exercises perfect. She didn't know what Madame was talking about. She was doing the exercises the same way she always had, and Madame had never found fault with them before. What could be wrong?

"How was rehearsal today?" Mrs. Gilbert asked when Patty walked in the door. On Mondays, Wednesdays, and Thursdays, Mrs. Gilbert left work early so that she could be there when Patty and Jana came home. The rest of the week, the girls were on their own until about six o'clock.

Patty shrugged and put her dance bag on the stairs leading to the second floor. "OK."

"Just OK? Not terrific?" Her mother smiled, looking up from the book she was reading.

"It was boring," Patty said. "We went through everything in slow motion—we barely even danced."

"Well, I'm sure Madame Baril knows what she's doing," Mrs. Gilbert said. "You have plenty of time to pick up the pace later. Do you want a snack?"

"No thanks." Patty looked at her dance bag. "I think I'm going to do some stretches downstairs for a while. My muscles still feel a little tight."

"I'll call you when dinner's ready," her mother said.

Patty grabbed her bag and went down to the basement, where her parents had built a ministudio for her. The small room contained a barre and a full-length mirror, but the floor didn't have the same spring as the one in Madame Baril's studio. Patty mostly stretched and worked on her alignment there. She shut the door and changed back into her ballet outfit. She put some slow piano music on her tape player, hoping it would help her relax.

The truth was, her first rehearsal for *Swan Lake* hadn't gone well at all. Madame had paid so much attention to her that it had made her nervous. When it was finally her turn to dance, her legs felt as though they were made of cement. Her *pirouettes* had been sloppy, and she'd messed up on her *arabesques*, too.

Patty stood in front of the mirror, examining her reflection. She lifted her leg slowly in an *arabesque*, opening her arms, then turning sideways. It felt the same as it always had. Did it look any different?

"Hey, ballet star, are you in there?" Jana knocked on the door.

"Come on in," Patty said. She turned down the piano music as her sister walked in.

"How'd it go today? Do you feel like a swan yet?" Jana asked.

Patty frowned. "Not exactly. Jana, have you noticed anything different about me lately?"

"No, I don't think so," Jana replied. "What do you mean?"

"Well, don't tell Mom or Dad, but Madame Baril said she thought there was something a little *off* about me today. What do you think she meant?"

Jana shrugged. "Beats me. You look the same— thin, pretty, you know, your average ballerina type."

Patty smiled. Jana always knew how to make her feel better. "Then why do you think she said it?"

"Maybe she forgot her glasses today," Jana said.

"She doesn't wear glasses," Patty said.

Jana examined her critically. "Maybe you're a little taller," she said.

"That must be it!" Patty cried. She ran past Jana, up to the kitchen, where their parents kept a record of their heights on the wall. "Measure me, Mom," she said, standing against the wall.

"What, hon?" Mrs. Gilbert was cutting vegetables on a board, and tossing them into a skillet.

"Measure me," Patty said. "I need to know if I've grown any."

"Right this minute?" Mrs. Gilbert asked. Patty nodded eagerly. Her mother wiped off her hands and got the ruler from a drawer under the counter. She put it on Patty's head and marked the spot on the wall in pencil.

Patty stepped away from the wall and looked at the mark. "Oh no! I grew!"

Mrs. Gilbert laughed. "There's nothing wrong with growing, honey."

"There is if you want to be a ballet dancer," Patty said. "Now I know what Madame Baril was talking about. I'm getting too tall."

"That's ridiculous," Jana said. She had followed Patty up the stairs and into the kitchen. "You're not tall at all."

"Yes, but I've grown this much in the last six months." Patty held up her fingers to indicate the distance between her marks on the wall. It was at least an inch. "If I keep growing like that, I'm going to be too tall soon."

"It's probably just a little growth spurt," Mrs. Gilbert said. "Jana went through one when she was your age, and look at her. She's not tall."

"Oh, thanks, Mom. Are you saying I'm a shrimp?" Jana asked with a grin. "Because if I am, then you're one, too." She went over and stood next to her mother. They were exactly the same height.

Patty shook her head. They didn't understand. If she kept growing, she was going to be too tall to become a classical ballerina. That must be what Madame had seen today in class.

"Honestly, Patty, I wouldn't worry," Mrs. Gilbert said. "You're still petite for your age. You won't turn into a giant overnight."

"You're just getting too wrapped up in this performance," Jana said. "Come watch a movie with me before dinner. That'll take your mind off it."

Patty followed her sister into the living room and slumped down on the couch. How was she supposed to take her mind off the only thing that mattered to her?

Three

"Where is everybody?" Mandy asked Jessica impatiently. They were sitting at a table in the lunchroom after school on Tuesday, waiting for people to show up for the first organizational meeting of the dance-marathon committee. Mandy was drumming her pencil against the table, and the noise was driving Jessica crazy.

"How should I know?" Jessica said. "You told everyone it was today, didn't you?"

Mandy nodded. "Well, here comes Lila, anyway."

Lila walked up to them, but she didn't sit down. "I just came to say I can't stick around today," she said. "I have to go home. My next-door neighbors, the Pratts, are moving out, and I have to say goodbye."

Mandy frowned. "Can't you see them later?"

Lila shook her head. "This is their last day. They sold the house and the new people are moving in next week."

"Really?" Jessica asked. "Do you know who they are yet?"

"No, but whoever they are, they have to be rich," Lila said. "The Pratt mansion is one of the biggest in the neighborhood. Their pool is even bigger than ours, and they have a huge guest house and six tennis courts. It's like a little country club. I told Daddy we should sell our boring old house and move in there."

In Jessica's opinion, Lila's luxurious home was far from boring, but she didn't want to tell Lila that. "Maybe they'll have a cute son who plays tennis," she said instead.

"I hope so," Lila said. "I'm sick of all the old fogies in my neighborhood. Anyway, I have to go. Good luck with your meeting."

"Don't you have any suggestions about music?" Mandy called after her.

"Just make sure it's good," Lila called over her shoulder as she walked out the door.

"Oh, that was a lot of help," Mandy said, throwing up her hands. "If no one else shows up, we're going to have to choose all the music ourselves. Then everyone's going to complain about it and—"

"Wait a second, here comes a whole bunch of people," Jessica said. About fifteen people had walked into the lunchroom, led by Janet Howell. "Hi, Janet," Jessica said happily. "Hi, everybody." Janet was the president of the Unicorns and one of the most important girls in school. Jessica knew that if Janet was behind the marathon, it couldn't help but be a success.

"Hi," Janet said. "I have some bad news."

"What's wrong?" Mandy asked.

"I failed my English test yesterday, and my parents said they were going to ground me for the next four weekends," Janet said.

"You're kidding!" Jessica said. "But that means you won't be able to dance in the marathon."

Janet nodded. "I know. Isn't it a total drag?"

"I can't be in the marathon either," Caroline Pearce said. "I found out my grandmother is coming to visit that weekend."

"My dad got tickets to a football game in Los Angeles that day," Tom McKay said with an apologetic shrug. "Sorry." He turned and walked out of the lunchroom.

Mandy crossed Tom's and Caroline's names off the list of volunteers.

For the next ten minutes, Jessica and Mandy sat there listening to the rest of the people explain why they couldn't be in the marathon after all, even though they'd only signed up yesterday.

"Is it just me, or was that incredibly suspicious?" Mandy asked once everyone had gone. "I mean, we find out we're going to have to dance for eleven and a half hours, and the next thing you know, everyone has plans that Saturday."

"I guess no one wants to dance for that long," Jessica said.

"This is a disaster." Mandy looked down at the list of participants. "We're down to eight people—all girls."

"I don't think that's going to make for a very exciting TV show," Jessica said glumly.

"Well, I'm not giving up this easily," Mandy said. "We'll figure out something."

Jessica stood up. "Well, there's no sense in sitting around here by ourselves. Let's go get a sundae at the Dairi Burger."

As they walked out of the building, Jessica was thinking hard. She needed to come up with a way to get everyone excited about the marathon again.

Suddenly she was struck with a great idea. If she could *promise* everyone that they'd be on TV, she was sure they would all want to participate.

I'll find a way to get Hollywood Jones to promise he'll come, she thought determinedly. *Then Janet and the others will be fighting for a chance to be in the marathon!*

*   *   *

"Patty, you're not getting the elevation you need. You must spring off your leg, like so," Madame Baril leaped into the air, her arms held perfectly above her head.

Patty knew that that was what she was supposed to do. She'd seen the step done a thousand times, and she'd done it a thousand times herself. But for some reason, she just couldn't get it right today.

"Now, try it again," Madame Baril instructed. Patty ran across the studio and jumped as high as she could. She could feel Madame's eyes following her every move.

When she landed, Madame Baril walked over to her. "Patty, perhaps you did not stretch enough today. You seem very stiff."

Patty nodded. "I think that must be it."

"Go over to the barre and run through a few warm-up exercises, then come back to me. And for heaven's sake, take off that sweater," Madame said, plucking at Patty's sleeve.

Patty fiddled with the tie on her light-pink wraparound sweater. "I'm cold," she said. "Can I keep it on?"

"Cold? After half an hour of dancing?" Madame reached out and touched Patty's forehead. "I hope you're not coming down with anything."

"Oh, no. I feel fine," Patty said. In fact, she was very hot inside her sweater, but she didn't want to take it off. She didn't want Madame to study her body and find anything wrong with her. She went over to the barre and listened vaguely as Madame instructed the other girls on their parts in the scene. Patty was working on her *developpés*, concentrating on unfolding her leg slowly and gracefully.

Suddenly, Madame Baril was at her side again. "Patty, stand up straight," she said. "What has happened to your line?"

What happened, Patty thought, *is that I grew too much!* But she didn't say anything. She'd been hunching over all day, hoping Madame wouldn't notice how tall she'd become. But she should have known that nothing would escape Madame's eye.

"Better," Madame said, nodding as she watched Patty's next *developpé*. "Stop for a minute, Patty. I want to talk to you."

Patty looked into her teacher's eyes. *Here it comes*, she thought, her stomach clenching into a tiny knot. *She's going to tell me that I'm too big to be the Swan Queen.* She followed Madame Baril over to the corner of the room.

"I think I know what's bothering you," Madame said when they were out of earshot of the others.

"You—you do?" Patty asked.

"Yes. You have been dancing poorly these past few days because there is something on your mind. And I think I know what that is." Madame paused, and Patty shifted nervously from foot to foot. "This is your first big starring role, isn't it?"

Patty nodded.

"Well, it's only natural to be nervous about that. I remember how I felt the first time I danced the role of Odette." Madame Baril looked almost dreamy for a second. "I was very happy to have the part—but very scared, too. I soon found out that there's only one thing to do."

"What's that?" Patty asked.

"Put it out of your mind," Madame Baril said. "Don't think about the performance, just think about your rehearsal. Pretend there isn't going to be a performance, and that you are only dancing for yourself. That is how you must always think, if you want to be a great dancer."

"And you think that will work—for me, I mean?" Patty had never felt so relieved. Madame Baril didn't want to get rid of her. She didn't think anything was wrong with Patty except a case of jangled nerves.

"Of course it will," Madame said. "But you must start right away. We can't afford to waste any of this precious rehearsal time. Do you understand?"

Patty nodded. "I'll try not to be so nervous tomorrow."

"Do better than that," Madame Baril said. "Promise yourself you will not be."

*   *   *

"So how are the rehearsals going?" Jessica asked. It was Tuesday afternoon, and she had just run into Kerry Glenn in the hallway of the dance studio.

"Pretty good," Kerry said. "How's class with Madame Andre?"

"She's as tough as ever." Jessica smiled. "Don't you miss her?" Kerry had moved from Jessica's class to the more advanced one just a few months ago.

"Believe it or not, Madame Baril is even harder," Kerry said, rubbing her thigh. "You should have seen how tough she was on Patty Gilbert today. I really felt bad for her."

"Well, I'm kind of glad I started dance lessons again, even if Madame Andre's class is a lot of work," Jessica said. "I'm going to be in great shape for the dance marathon." *Or what's left of it, anyway*, she added silently. "You're still going to dance in it, aren't you?"

"Sure thing. I wouldn't miss it for the world," Kerry said. "I think Jo and Tina are going to come, too."

"Great," Jessica said. "What about Patty?"

"I haven't really had a chance to ask her," Kerry said. "I think she's still inside, if you want to try to catch her."

"OK, I will. See you later, Kerry. I can't wait to see you guys dance *Swan Lake*." Jessica waved at

Kerry and walked down the hall and into the changing room. She spotted Patty sitting at the far end of a bench, pulling on her socks and shoes. "Hi," Jessica said, walking over to her. "How's rehearsal going?"

Patty looked up. "OK."

"I'm Jessica, by the way."

"I know," Patty said. She got up and started to pack up her dance bag.

"I didn't want you to confuse me with my sister," Jessica explained. "I have an identical twin, you know."

"I know," Patty said. She didn't smile.

Patty sure isn't much of a conversationalist, Jessica thought. But then she reminded herself that she was talking to her for a good cause. She cleared her throat. "Uh, I wanted to ask you if you felt like helping with the dance marathon we're trying to organize at school. Do you think you could come and dance for a few hours?"

"I heard about that," Patty said. "I don't know. I don't think it would be a good idea, with my performance coming up and all."

"You wouldn't have to dance long," Jessica said. "Even half an hour would help. Besides, Hollywood Jones is coming." It wasn't really a lie, she figured, because she was going to make sure he did.

"I don't know." Patty put her ballet shoes into the outside pocket of her bag. "I'll think about it."

"Well, OK." Jessica didn't know what else to say.

"I have to get going or I'll miss my bus," Patty said. She walked out of the room without even saying goodbye.

Four

◇

"What should we say to get him to come?" Mandy asked. She and Jessica were sitting at the Wakefields' kitchen table Thursday afternoon, drafting a letter to Hollywood Jones.

"Tell him that Sweet Valley Middle School is a great place," Jessica said. She paused, thinking of Mrs. Arnette yelling at her that morning for being late to social studies. "Well, some of the time, anyway. And tell him all the kids are really cool." A picture came into her mind of Randy Mason ballroom dancing in gym class. "Well, not all of them. Most of them, though."

"No, we have to be more serious," Mandy said. "We don't want him to think we're flaky. We should sound really interesting and smart."

"Good luck," said Steven, Jessica's older brother, as he walked into the kitchen.

Jessica stuck out her tongue at him.

Steven grabbed some cookies from the jar on the counter and came over to the table. "What are you guys doing?" He shoved two of the cookies into his mouth.

"Writing a letter," Jessica said. "By the way, Steven, you're supposed to chew food before you swallow it."

"Who are you writing to—Johnny Buck?" Steven pretended to swoon. "Dear Johnny, I absolutely *loooove* your music. You are *soooooo* cute."

"We are not writing to Johnny Buck," Mandy said, frowning at him. "We're writing to Holly-wood Jones."

Steven grabbed another cookie. "Dear Holly-wood, we think your sideburns are so gorgeous. Do you think you could send us one of them?" He laughed so hard that he had to hold on to the edge of the counter for support.

"Cut it out, this is serious," Jessica said. "The show is coming to Sweet Valley and we want to get on it."

"Doing what?" Steven asked.

"We're having a dance marathon," Mandy told him.

"No kidding." Steven nodded. "So you and your boyfriend what's-his-name are going to dance the night away together, huh? What is his name, anyway? Airhead?"

"It's Aaron," Jessica said, glaring at him. "Steven, go away."

"Why didn't you just say so?" Steven grabbed another handful of cookies from the jar and went upstairs.

Jessica looked at Mandy and rolled her eyes. "Let's not mention Steven in this letter, or Hollywood Jones will probably cancel his trip to Sweet Valley completely."

Mandy laughed. "OK, so what *should* we talk about?"

"Tell him how exciting the marathon is going to be. You know, how long we're going to dance, and how a ton of people are going to be doing it," Jessica said.

Mandy wrote for a minute, then stopped. "How many people *are* doing it?"

Jessica glanced down at the list on the table. Still only eight girls. "Tell him fifty."

"But there aren't anywhere near that many people signed up," Mandy protested.

"Not yet there aren't," Jessica said. "But once Hollywood agrees to come, there will be."

Mandy looked at her suspiciously. "Jess, isn't this kind of backward? We're telling him tons of people are signed up, so he'll come, so tons of people will sign up."

Jessica smiled. "Exactly! Brilliant, huh?" She

looked down at the list again. "Better make it a hundred people."

By the time rehearsal started on Friday, Patty was beginning to feel confident about her dancing again. After her talk with Madame Baril, she'd been able to relax and dance almost as well as she had in the audition. Of course, Madame Baril was still difficult and demanding, but that was normal.

Patty walked out of the changing room and into the studio, thinking about how beautiful her costume was going to be. The seamstress had measured her the day before for the fluffy white tutu and feather headdress. Just imagining herself in the costume was enough to give Patty goose bumps. *Finally, it's all coming together!* she thought. Opening night was only two weeks away.

"Hi," Kerry greeted her when she entered the studio.

Patty was in such a good mood, she replied right away, without even thinking about it. "Hi, Kerry." She smiled at her classmate.

"I like your leg warmers," Kerry said. She pointed at Patty's legs—she was wearing pink and black striped leg warmers over her white tights.

"Thanks," Patty said. "My sister gave them to me for my birthday last year."

"I didn't know you had a sister," Kerry said. "How old is she?" She sat down and started doing some stretches.

"Sixteen. She's a junior at Sweet Valley High," Patty said. "Her name's Jana."

"That's a pretty name." Kerry put one leg behind her and leaned forward to touch her knee.

Patty nodded. She leaned over to retie one of her shoe ribbons.

"I have two sisters," Kerry said. "One's younger and—"

"Patty, may I have a word with you?"

Patty looked up, startled to see Madame Baril standing at her side. She hadn't even heard the teacher come in.

"Sure," Patty said. She pulled up her leg warmers. "What is it?"

"Come into my office, will you?" Madame Baril asked. She turned and walked across the studio. "We will begin in five minutes," she announced to the rest of the class.

Patty glanced down at Kerry, who shrugged. Patty didn't like the serious tone in Madame's voice, but she told herself there was nothing to worry about.

Madame Baril's office walls were covered with photographs of famous dancers. Just looking at them made Patty feel good about being a dancer. There was a picture of Madame Baril at twenty years old, being partnered by one of the most famous male dancers in the world at the time. Patty loved that picture. Madame Baril had been so beautiful.

Madame sat down behind her big desk and gestured for Patty to sit opposite her. "Patty, I've seen a lot of improvement in your dancing in the past few days."

Patty nodded. "Thank you."

"But something's still bothering me," Madame Baril continued. Patty felt her stomach tighten. "I'm not quite sure what it is, but I think it has something to do with your alignment."

"My alignment?" Patty repeated. She pulled nervously at one of her leg warmers.

"Yes." Madame leaned forward in her chair and studied Patty's face. "It's not quite as even as it used to be."

Patty didn't know what to say. She didn't even understand what Madame was trying to tell her. "Do you mean that my technique has gotten worse?"

"No," Madame said. "It's not that. I've been seeing something different about your posture. It doesn't seem quite straight. I noticed it again just now while you were bending over to tie your shoe."

Patty didn't understand what Madame was getting at. As far as Patty knew, her posture was perfect. In fact, everyone was always complimenting her on it.

"Would you mind having your doctor check it out?" Madame Baril asked.

"But . . . there's nothing wrong with me,"

Patty said. "This isn't because I'm getting too tall, is it?" she asked. "Maybe I just look funny to you because I grew a little."

"Too tall?" Madame Baril shook her head. "No, it's not that."

Patty heaved a sigh of relief. "I thought you were going to tell me I was too tall to be the Swan Queen."

"Nonsense! If anything, it helps you. The Swan Queen must have a strong and dramatic presence," Madame Baril said. "Your height is perfectly acceptable, Patty. I just—well, I'd like you to see a doctor. Perhaps it's nothing—it may all be in my head. Still, I wouldn't feel comfortable if you didn't go."

Patty squirmed in her seat. She didn't want to go to the doctor. She knew there wasn't anything wrong with her. She'd feel it if there was.

"Patty, I am afraid I must ask you to do this," Madame Baril said. "Promise me you will take care of it over the weekend."

Patty bit her lip. She couldn't disobey Madame. "OK, I'll go to the doctor," she said. "But I feel perfectly fine."

Madame nodded.

"You're going to let me rehearse today, aren't you?" asked Patty.

Madame Baril smiled. "That's what I like about you, Patty. You're a born performer. Nothing will keep you from dancing." She got up from her desk.

That's right, Patty thought as she followed Madame Baril back down the hall to the studio. *Nothing will keep me from dancing.*

Patty stood in front of her mirror in the basement. She turned to the side and examined her reflection. She couldn't see anything different about her posture. She leaned over, stretching to touch her toes. Nothing.

She ran upstairs and knocked on Jana's door. "Can I come in?"

"Sure," Jana called. When Patty walked in, Jana turned around from her desk. "What's up? Don't tell me you're still rehearsing—it's nine o'clock!"

"No, I was just . . . well, remember when I asked if you noticed anything strange about me?" Patty asked.

Jana nodded. "And you decided you were turning into a basketball player."

Patty smiled in spite of her worry. "Right. Madame Baril talked to me about it again today." She took a deep breath. "She said my posture looks funny. Does it look funny to you?"

"Patty, you could walk from here to San Francisco with a whole stack of books balanced on your head," Jana said. "Your posture's perfect."

"That's what I thought, too," Patty said. "But she said it's not quite straight or something."

Jana looked puzzled. "She's probably just

hyper about the performance. Don't let it get to you."

Patty wondered if she should tell Jana that Madame wanted her to see a doctor. But she decided not to mention it. The whole thing was ridiculous. If nothing hurt, how could something be wrong?

"Well, thanks," Patty said. "I guess you're right. I'm going to finish my homework."

"I hope you have better luck with yours than I'm having with mine," Jana said with a groan as she turned back to her textbook.

Before Patty went to her room, she hurried downstairs to the den and grabbed a volume of her father's medical encyclopedia off the shelf. Upstairs, she closed her door and sat down on her bed. She flipped through the thick book, looking at diagrams of muscles and nerves and a detailed illustration of a human skeleton.

But the book only explained how everything worked—not how it didn't work if something went wrong. Patty didn't know what to look up to find out what Madame Baril thought was wrong with her.

There was a knock on the door, and her mother stuck her head into the room. "How are you doing on your homework?"

Patty slammed the encyclopedia shut and shoved it to the corner of her desk. She pretended to be concentrating on a math problem. "Pretty good so far, Mom."

Mrs. Gilbert took a few steps closer to Patty's desk. "I'll bet it's hard to concentrate on math when you have *Swan Lake* on your mind."

Patty nodded. It *was* hard to concentrate, but not for the reasons her mother thought. Patty was still trying to decide whether to ask her parents to take her to the doctor over the weekend. If they did, and the doctor found out something was wrong, like Madame thought, then what?

"No way—did Randy Mason really say that?" Belinda asked, laughing.

It was Saturday afternoon, and a bunch of the Unicorns were wandering around the Valley Mall.

Lila nodded, looking disgusted. "He said he wants to dance with me all night, and if he can't, he's not going to do it."

"He'd better do it," Jessica said. "We told Hollywood Jones we were going to have a hundred people."

"Well, *you* dance with Randy then," Lila said. "I'd rather keep my toes."

"Not to mention your reputation," Grace Oliver added.

"Hey, check out that shirt," Ellen exclaimed. She rushed over to a nearby store window.

"Wait a minute. Look at *this*." Mandy pointed to a sign posted in the window. "I can't believe it!"

Jessica looked where Mandy was pointing and saw a bright pink sign with big blue letters. "WE

NEED YOU," she read aloud. "Come to Big Mesa Middle School and be on TV! We need as many people as possible to be in our all-school three-legged race!"

"A three-legged race? They think they're going to get on *You'll Never Believe This!* by running around with their legs tied together?" Lila scoffed.

"They're going to look ridiculous," Tamara Chase said.

"Yeah, but you know, that show goes for that kind of thing," Kimberly said. "They love to show people making idiots of themselves."

"True," Ellen said.

"The point is, how are they so sure they're going to be on TV?" Mandy asked.

"They must have written to the station, just like we did," Jessica said. "Maybe they got an answer already."

"We can't let some Big Mesa kids get on the show instead of us," Belinda said.

"Don't worry," Jessica said. "We'll get on the show." She noticed a flyer lying on the ground nearby, picked it up, and stuffed it in her pocket.

Five

◇

"Patty, did you go to the doctor?" Madame Baril asked when Patty walked into rehearsal on Monday afternoon.

"Yes," Patty said nervously. "She said there's nothing wrong with me." She walked over to the barre and started doing some warm-up stretches.

"Really?" Madame Baril seemed surprised. "What sort of examination did she give you?"

"Oh, the usual," Patty said, beginning a series of *pliés*. "She checked everything."

"She did?" Madame Baril said. "Like what?"

"She took my pulse and listened to my heartbeat and all that," Patty said.

"Did she check your joints and bones?"

Patty nodded. "She looked at everything. She said I was in good shape."

"And there are no problems?" Madame asked.

"Right," Patty said. She took a deep breath. She didn't know how much longer she could keep on lying to Madame Baril. It was making her feel terrible.

"Madame Baril?" Constance, the seamstress who was sewing their costumes for the performance, was standing in the doorway. "I hope it's all right if I come by now. I wanted to check the fittings on the girls."

Patty heaved a sigh of relief.

"This is a good time. We still have fifteen minutes before rehearsals begin," Madame Baril said. "Who did you need to see?"

"Well, all the girls." Constance walked into the studio, carrying a box full of half-finished costumes. "Since Patty's here, I can start with her."

Patty smiled and walked over to Constance. "You can slip this on over your leotard for now," Constance said, pulling Patty's costume out of the box. "I just want to check the length and see the overall effect. We'll have a final fitting later."

Patty nodded and stepped into the beautiful white tutu. She admired the silky fabric as she pulled it up around her.

"Of course, when it's finished, I'll add lots of material to make you look more like a swan," Constance said, smoothing the costume around Patty's shoulders. "You're going to look so pretty."

"Patty will make a beautiful swan," Madame Baril agreed.

"OK, everything looks good," Constance said. "You can take it off now."

Patty stepped out of the costume, being careful not to bend over at the waist. It seemed that whenever she did that lately, Madame Baril made comments about her posture.

"Girls!" Madame clapped her hands together. "Come over here. Constance needs to check your costumes."

Jo, Tina, Kerry, and several other girls came hurrying over. "Wow, is that your costume?" Jo asked, touching Patty's tutu. "It's so pretty!"

Patty smiled. "Thanks."

"Could you slip this on?" Constance asked Tina. "I need to make sure it's the right length on you."

"Patty, I'd like to talk to you," Madame Baril said.

Again? Patty thought. "I—I really want to do some extra stretching before class," she said.

The look Madame gave her reminded Patty why she had been told never to contradict her ballet teacher. She could see the others staring at her, too, as if she had lost her mind. "But my exercises can wait, of course," she added quickly.

Madame nodded and guided Patty to a corner

of the room. Patty could feel the other girls looking at her.

"Patty, there's a story I want to tell you. It's about an old friend of mine, a girl I went to ballet school with in New York," Madame Baril began. "Her name was Camille. We came into the school together when we were fifteen. I don't mind saying that the two of us were in the top of our class from the time we entered until our third and final year there. Camille and I always competed for the top roles. We danced together, we shared a dormitory room, and we were great friends.

"Well, in our third year, the school decided it would produce *The Sleeping Beauty.* Camille got the part of the Fairy of Modesty, which requires a very demanding solo. She had heard that several important people from the ballet world would be attending the performance, which would mark the twenty-fifth anniversary of the school.

"Camille was very nervous—she wanted to find a place with a company, and she thought that if she could impress someone with her performance, she would have made a good start. However, during the early stages of rehearsal, she twisted her ankle. I could see that it was swollen, but she wouldn't admit that it was still bothering her. She ignored it, dancing on it every day, even though it was hurting her so much that she cried herself to sleep at night.

"Finally, the night of the performance came.

Camille wanted only to last through it, then she promised herself she would see a doctor. But do you know what happened? She went into her first jump, and when she landed, she collapsed, right in the middle of the stage.''

Patty gasped. "What happened?''

"Her ankle was broken, of course,'' Madame said. "She had to stay off it for months. When she came back, she was never the dancer she had once been. She was all right, but she could never regain her confidence.''

"That's terrible,'' Patty said.

"Yes, it was,'' Madame agreed. "But you, thankfully, are in perfect health.'' She brushed some rosin off her hands, then stared directly into Patty's eyes. "You can see that after an experience like that, I want to be very cautious with my pupils. Especially pupils that have a great deal of promise. I am very relieved I don't have to worry about you.''

Madame Baril walked off to check on the other girls' costumes, and Patty leaned against the wall. She was shaking all over. Madame Baril was right. A ballerina had to be careful about her health. She didn't know what could be wrong with her, but she had to trust Madame's judgement and find out. She knew one thing—she didn't want to end up like Camille.

*   *   *

"Hello, is Brittany Shaw there?" Jessica asked. She glanced at the flyer she had taken from the mall. She was standing in the upstairs hallway after school on Monday.

"This is Brittany," the girl who answered the phone replied.

"Oh, hi," Jessica said. "I'm calling about your flyer for the three-legged race."

"Great!" Brittany said. "Do you want to sign up?"

"Well, um, that depends," Jessica said. "Are you sure it's going to be on TV?"

"Pretty sure," Brittany said. "We got a letter from Hollywood Jones. He said he'd come by sometime next Saturday afternoon, so we're just going to be ready and waiting."

"How many people do you have signed up so far?" Jessica asked. She couldn't imagine too many people being psyched about hopping across a field.

"A hundred and forty-six," Brittany said. "Why, do you need a partner? I'm sure we could find one for you. What's your name? I'll put you on the list."

"No, that's OK," Jessica said. "Thanks." She hung up the phone and slumped against the wall. A hundred and forty-six people? She'd told Hollywood Jones they were only going to have a hundred—and even that was stretching the truth by ninety-two people! Jessica knew that she'd better think of another plan to make the dance marathon successful—and fast.

"Patty, did you remember to ask about getting extra tickets for your performance?" Mr. Gilbert asked Monday night at dinner. "I told Andrew and Erica we'd pick up a pair for them."

Patty shook her head. "Sorry, I forgot."

"Well, that's OK. There's still plenty of time." Patty's father handed her a bowl of salad. "How was rehearsal today?"

"Actually, that was what I wanted to talk to you about," Patty said.

"Don't tell us," Jana said. "Someone from the Los Angeles Ballet dropped by and wants you to dance for them." She grinned at her sister as she passed a pitcher of iced tea across the table to her.

"I wouldn't be surprised if someone from the company was at your performance, Patty," Mrs. Gilbert said.

"Mom, please," Patty said. Why were they making this so hard for her? Usually it was fun to sit around and dream about her future, but tonight it was getting on her nerves. "I'm a long way from being in a company."

"It sounds as if you're feeling tense about the performance," Mr. Gilbert said. He took a sip of iced tea.

"This chicken is great, Mom," Jana said.

"Wait a minute," Mr. Gilbert protested. "I made the chicken."

Jana laughed. "I know, Dad. I was just trying to give you a hard time."

Patty couldn't hold it in any longer. "I have to go to the doctor tomorrow," she blurted out.

Her parents and sister turned to stare at her. "What?" Mrs. Gilbert asked.

"Why?" Mr. Gilbert said. "What's wrong?"

Looking at the concerned expressions on their faces, Patty knew she couldn't tell them that Madame Baril was worried about her. "Nothing's wrong," she said quickly. "Madame Baril wants me to be checked out, that's all."

She saw her parents exchange worried glances. "Are all the girls being checked?" Mr. Gilbert asked.

"No," Patty said. "It's just because, well, because my role is so much more demanding. She's big on checking everything out, I guess, just in case."

"I don't get it," Jana said. "I mean, you go to the doctor every year. What's she going to find out that would have anything to do with dancing?"

Patty shrugged. "Beats me. She just asked me to go. You know Madame Baril. She gets these ideas and she won't take no for an answer."

"When do you need to go?" Mrs. Gilbert asked.

"Tomorrow, before rehearsal," Patty said.

"I'm not sure we'll be able to get an appointment," Mrs. Gilbert said. "That's pretty short notice."

"Mom, I have to," Patty said. "Otherwise she won't let me dance!"

"Well, in that case, I'm sure Doctor Ringwald can squeeze you in," Mrs. Gilbert said. "Just a regular physical, right?"

"Right," Patty said. "Then Madame will know I'm ready for the performance."

Six

"Come on in, Patty," Dr. Ringwald said with a smile as she opened the door to her office.

Patty looked at her mother.

"It's OK, honey. I'll wait right here for you," Mrs. Gilbert said.

Patty nodded and got up from her chair in the waiting room. Dr. Ringwald was about thirty years old, with short black hair and gold wire-rimmed glasses. Since Patty had only lived in Sweet Valley for a year, she didn't know Dr. Ringwald very well, but she liked her—especially her sense of humor. Even when Patty had come in with a bad case of the flu the winter before, Dr. Ringwald had managed to make her laugh. She was a warm, friendly person, and Patty felt as if she could talk to her about anything.

"Your mother told me you need a quick checkup," Dr. Ringwald said, sitting down in her chair behind the desk. "Is there any special reason why? You're not scheduled for your regular checkup for another four months."

Patty sat on the edge of the seat facing her. "I'm going to be in a ballet," she said.

"Hey, that's terrific," Dr. Ringwald said. "Which one?"

"*Swan Lake*," Patty said. "My teacher, Madame Baril, wanted me to have a checkup before the performance."

Dr. Ringwald leaned forward in her chair and rested her arms on her desk. "Why is that?"

Patty shrugged. "I don't know. She thinks maybe there's something wrong with me. She said my posture was a little off. I feel perfectly fine, though—I think maybe I look a little funny to her because I'm getting taller. She's really picky."

Dr. Ringwald nodded. "I took ballet once, too, if you can believe that. I was so ungraceful that they named a new step after me—the Ringwald Rump Landing."

Patty giggled.

"They're real sticklers for posture in ballet, I remember that much," Dr. Ringwald said. "Well, let's try something. First I want to measure you to see how much you've grown." She stepped over to the chart on the wall, and Patty stood against it. The doctor made a note on her clipboard, then looked at Patty's chart. "You're right, you have been getting taller. An inch and a quarter in eight months!"

"I knew it," Patty said, shaking her head. "I knew that's all it was."

"Let's try something else before we say that for sure." Dr. Ringwald set her clipboard on her desk. "Could you touch your toes for me, please?"

Patty hesitated. That was what had gotten her in here in the first place.

"You're a ballet dancer, so I know you can touch your toes," Dr. Ringwald said. "You should see some of the kids I get in here!" She made a funny face and hunched over, her fingertips dangling just to her knees.

A smile spread across Patty's face. She *was* proud of being as limber as she was. She reached down slowly and let her fingers touch the floor.

Dr. Ringwald pressed her hands against Patty's back. "I'm just feeling your spine," she said. "I want to make sure everything's in order."

"How could it get out of order?" Patty asked. She expected Dr. Ringwald to laugh, but the doctor didn't say anything. She just kept touching Patty's back, starting at her neck and working her way down. Then she stopped, and Patty stood up.

"No, go back down, please," Dr. Ringwald said.

Patty bent over again. This time, Dr. Ringwald

stood off to one side, watching her. "OK, you can straighten up."

"What next?" asked Patty, sitting on the edge of the examination table.

Dr. Ringwald sat down behind her desk and made a few notes on Patty's chart. "Would you ask your mother to come in for a minute, please?" she asked.

"You mean I'm finished?" Patty hopped off the table.

Dr. Ringwald nodded.

"Great." Patty opened the door and went out into the waiting room. "Mom, Dr. Ringwald wants to see you now."

"That was fast," Mrs. Gilbert said as she got to her feet. "Is everything OK?"

Patty nodded eagerly. "I guess so. She hardly looked at me at all."

"Don't we pay the bill out here?" Mrs. Gilbert asked.

"I don't know. She wants you to go in," Patty said, sitting down.

Dr. Ringwald stuck her head out of her office. "Patty, I want you to come, too," she said.

Patty shrugged. She probably just wanted to talk about her growth spurt, or becoming a teenager or something.

When she and her mother walked into the office, Dr. Ringwald gestured to a couple of chairs near her desk. "Have a seat," she said.

"What's the report?" asked Mrs. Gilbert. "Is Patty ready for her debut?"

Dr. Ringwald fiddled with the pen in her hand. "Yes, but I'm afraid I have some bad news."

Patty's eyes widened, and she glanced anxiously at her mother. How could there be bad news? Dr. Ringwald had only checked her for about two minutes.

"Patty mentioned that her ballet teacher had commented on her posture, that perhaps it wasn't quite the same as it used to be," Dr. Ringwald said.

"You didn't tell us that," Mrs. Gilbert said, turning to Patty.

Patty didn't say anything. She was so nervous she could barely breathe.

"So the first thing I did was give Patty a routine screening for scoliosis," Dr. Ringwald went on. "Patty, scoliosis is the medical term for curvature of the spine. If your spine becomes curved, it can affect your posture—the way you stand, the way you look."

"My mother had scoliosis," Mrs. Gilbert said. "Are you saying—does Patty—"

"Yes. I'm afraid she seems to have a fairly advanced case of it," Dr. Ringwald said. "Of course, I'll refer you to a specialist, an orthopedic surgeon, who will examine Patty more fully and determine what, if anything, needs to be done."

"A surgeon?" Mrs. Gilbert said. "Will Patty have to have surgery?"

"I really can't tell you that," Dr. Ringwald said. "That's not my area of expertise. However—"

"Then how do you know I have it?" Patty demanded. "Maybe you're wrong!"

Mrs. Gilbert put her hand on Patty's arm.

"Patty, I do this screening test every year on every child I see," Dr. Ringwald said patiently. "It's standard procedure for all doctors. Scoliosis usually strikes girls when they're just becoming teenagers, so we're extra careful about checking then."

"But you just saw Patty eight months ago," Mrs. Gilbert said. "How could it have come on so fast?"

"It can happen that way," Dr. Ringwald said. "Especially during growth spurts, like the one Patty's just had."

"So what's going to happen to me?" Patty asked.

"Patty, the curve may need to be corrected," Dr. Ringwald said. "If it isn't, your posture could get worse and worse."

"But no one's noticed it yet, except Madame Baril," Patty said. "And my back doesn't hurt or anything. Why can't I just stay the way I am?"

"What kind of treatments are there?" asked Mrs. Gilbert. "How do they correct a curve?"

"If it's not a serious curve, the doctor will probably watch it for a while. If it doesn't get much worse, he could leave it alone," Dr. Ringwald said.

"Otherwise, there are two basic options—wearing a brace, or having surgery."

Patty felt her heart drop into her stomach. "Did you say a brace?" She'd known a boy in her old school who had had to wear a brace on one of his legs. If she wore a brace, she wouldn't be able to dance anymore!

Dr. Ringwald nodded. "It's very effective. Of course, the orthopedist will be able to tell you much more about all the options." She scribbled a name and phone number on a piece of paper. "You should make an appointment as soon as possible. The earlier we catch these things, the better."

Out of the corner of her eye, Patty could see that Dr. Ringwald was looking at her sympathetically. But Patty didn't want Dr. Ringwald's sympathy. She wanted someone to tell her that this was all a dream—a horrible dream—and that when she woke up tomorrow, she'd be the same old Patty Gilbert, star of *Swan Lake.*

There was one thing she could do. She could pretend she'd never heard the word scoliosis. *No one has to know,* she thought. *Especially not Madame Baril!*

"Patty, are you with us today? We are on our *grands battements,* not our *battements frappés,*" Madame Baril scolded.

Patty snapped to attention, feeling her face turn hot with embarrassment. Here she was, supposedly the best dancer in the class, and she couldn't even keep up with simple barre exercises! She wanted to work as hard as she could—after all, she might not be dancing much longer, if the doctors had anything to say about it. Dr. Ringwald had said it was fine to continue with her class for now, but Patty was afraid that that might change soon.

"You are not getting much lift today," Madame said, standing and looking at Patty with her arms folded across her chest.

As class went on, Patty felt as if she was listening to a broken record of Madame Baril's voice yelling at her. "Patty, you are dancing like a robot!" "Patty, you need more elevation!" "Patty, where is the emotion?"

How could Patty explain that she was *all* emotion that day? It was taking every ounce of her strength just to keep from breaking down in front of everyone and telling them the truth.

When Madame Baril came over to her during a short break, Patty felt her whole body get tense.

"Patty, I don't know why you insist on wearing this huge baggy sweatshirt. I can't see your lines—I can't see you move," the teacher complained. "You know I prefer you to wear only a leotard during class."

Patty shrugged. "I know, but—" She was about to protest, but she saw the stern look in Madame's eye. "I'm sorry. I was wearing it to warm up and I forgot to take it off." Patty pulled the sweatshirt off over her head and tossed it in the corner. What did it matter—soon Madame Baril and everyone else would know the truth, anyway. Patty just wanted to hide her problem long enough to make it through *Swan Lake*.

She threw twice as much effort into the rest of the rehearsal.

After class, Patty was standing in the changing room, slowly taking off her leotard. She knew she should hurry and get home, but she couldn't help lingering, thinking about how much she was going to miss the dance studio.

Don't think that way, she told herself. *You might not have to give it up at all. Dr. Ringwald didn't say anything definite.*

She was pulling her long-sleeved T-shirt over her head when Kerry came around the corner from another row of lockers.

"Patty, I couldn't believe how much the Bear was getting on you today," Kerry said, shaking her head. She had let her long braid out of its bun, and it was swinging around her shoulders.

Patty shrugged. She put her foot up on the bench to tie the laces to her sneakers. "She's like that all the time."

"I don't know. If I were you, I'd be mad. She wasn't being fair," Kerry said.

"She wasn't?"

"No. There's nothing wrong with your *developpés*. I think they're absolutely perfect," Kerry said.

Patty knew that Kerry was trying to make her feel better, but for some reason, the compliment only made her feel worse. What if her *developpes* were perfect? Soon it wouldn't matter anymore.

"She's always demanding, but she's been getting downright ridiculous lately," Kerry said, shifting her dance bag from one shoulder to the other. "She's acting like we're going to be dancing at Lincoln Center or something."

Patty stuffed the rest of her things into her bag without answering Kerry. She was afraid that if she opened her mouth to speak, she'd burst into tears.

"Oh, well," Kerry said. "I guess she just wants us to do well. But if you ask me, you don't have to worry about anything. You're the best dancer in class. You'll probably be a professional ballerina someday."

"I have to go," Patty mumbled, striding past Kerry. She didn't dare look up at her. "See you tomorrow."

"Patty, wait up," Kerry called after her, as Patty ran out the door.

Patty didn't slow down. She ran out the front doors and down the sidewalk. Instead of heading home, she ran toward the park near her house. She knew it would be deserted at this time of day.

Patty didn't stop running until she got to the swingset. She threw her bag down on the ground and collapsed on a swing, putting her head into her hands and bursting into tears. "It's not fair," she mumbled between sobs, as the swing rocked gently back and forth. "I don't deserve this!"

She'd never felt so lonely and scared in her life.

Seven

◇

"Dear Miss Wakefield and Miss Miller," Jessica read out loud. It was Wednesday afternoon, and she and Elizabeth were sitting in the kitchen. "Thank you for your letter. We will be in Sweet Valley on the weekend you mentioned, and will try to stop by your school at the time you specified to see what you have planned. However, we cannot promise that you will be on the show. Thank you for your interest in our show. We look forward to seeing you."

"Who's we?" asked Elizabeth. "I thought you wrote to Hollywood Jones."

Jessica frowned, pointing to the signature. "It says, From the Creative Staff. Does that mean Hollywood will come or just some staff people?"

Elizabeth shrugged. "I don't know, Jessica. That letter doesn't sound very promising."

"I know," Jessica said. "I think I'm going to have to give Hollywood a call." She grabbed the phone from the wall and sat back down at the kitchen table.

"Are you serious? You're calling Hollywood Jones?" Elizabeth asked.

"Sure, why not?" Jessica punched in the phone number listed on the TV show's official stationery. "Hollywood Jones, please," she said into the receiver.

"Hollywood Jones's office," a man answered in a deep voice.

"Mr. Jones, is that really you?" Jessica asked.

"No, it's not," the man replied with a sigh. "That's why I said it was his office. My name is Brian. How may I help you?"

"Oh. Well, I'm calling from Sweet Valley. I wrote to tell him about what we're planning at my school, and I wanted to make sure he could come," Jessica explained. "He *is* coming, isn't he?"

"That depends. Who are you?"

"Jessica Wakefield. I'm in the middle school and—"

"Oh, yes, you're the ones doing the three-legged race," Brian said. "We're definitely coming to film you. Hollywood's very excited about it."

Jessica cleared her throat. "Uh, no, I'm from the

other middle school. We're doing the dance marathon, remember?"

"Oh. Right," Brian said. He suddenly sounded much less enthusiastic.

"When I wrote I only had a hundred people signed up," Jessica said. "That's why I'm calling. Now we have two hundred people doing it." She saw Elizabeth's eyes widen.

"Two hundred?"

"Uh huh."

"Well, that's really something. Let me check our list."

Jessica waited anxiously for his answer. *Please say yes*, she thought, crossing her fingers underneath the table.

"You know, Jessica, I think you may just get a visit from Hollywood himself," Brian said finally.

"All right!" Jessica cried.

"We'll let you know what time as soon as possible. We're still lining up events. Now, this doesn't necessarily mean you'll be on the show. You realize that, don't you?"

"Oh, yes, of course," Jessica said, a big grin on her face. She knew if she got Hollywood Jones to come to her school, she would find a way to make sure she ended up on TV.

"Jessica, you don't have two hundred people signed up," Elizabeth said when she hung up the phone. "You don't even have fifty."

"No, but we will," Jessica said confidently. "Just wait."

"Wow, I can't believe you talked to *the* Hollywood Jones," Kimberly said at lunch on Thursday. "What was he like?"

"He was totally friendly," Jessica said, waving her hand airily. "I told him all about our marathon and how we were going to have a huge crowd, and he said he would definitely come and film it." She could see Lila looking at her suspiciously. But Jessica didn't think it was necessary to tell her friends that she'd only talked to Hollywood's assistant.

"That's terrific," Mandy said.

"Yeah, he was really sweet." Jessica sighed dreamily. "Anyway, all we need to do now is let everyone know we're definitely going to be on TV, so there will be lots of people there."

"No problem," Grace said. "Once they hear about this, everyone will want to come."

"How many people do we still need?" Tamara asked.

Jessica poked a straw into her soda. "A hundred or so," she said casually.

"A *hundred*?" Lila exclaimed. "You told him we were going to have a *hundred* people?"

"Actually, I said two hundred," Jessica admitted. "It was the only way to get him to come. Big Mesa has a hundred and fifty people signed up already."

"I don't know what's going to be harder, dancing all day or finding all those people," Belinda said.

"Well, I'll be there for sure," Janet said. "You can put me on your list."

"I thought you were grounded," Mandy said.

"Oh, I was," Janet said. "But since, um, I studied all last weekend, my parents changed their minds."

"Likely story," Mandy whispered to Jessica, rolling her eyes.

"Everyone should try to get at least five people to sign up before they leave school today," Jessica said.

"Five people? That's impossible," Ellen complained.

"Do you want to be on TV or not?" Jessica asked. "I *promised* Hollywood, and he's going to be really mad if he gets here and the auditorium's empty." *And that's putting it mildly*, she added to herself.

"Patty, don't you want to get some lunch?" asked Ms. Luster, the school librarian.

"No, thank you," Patty said with a faint smile. "I need to do some research first."

"What kind of research?" asked Ms. Luster.

"Oh, it's . . . for science class," Patty said. "I just need to look up some stuff." She walked over to the reference books, hoping Ms. Luster would leave her alone. She didn't feel like talking to anybody.

She pulled one of the large science encyclopedia volumes off the shelf and looked up "scoliosis." She was surprised to find a whole section on it.

"Scoliosis, the lateral curvature of the spine, affects approximately one in every fifty preteen and teenage children," she read. "Depending on the degree of the curve, some of those will require treatment and some will not. The most common form of treatment is the wearing of the Milwaukee brace." There was a tiny illustration of a girl wearing the Milwaukee brace in the margin.

Patty couldn't believe her eyes. The brace went all the way from the girl's neck to below her rear end, surrounding her body like a big cage. Patty could never wear something like that. She wouldn't be able to move! All of her muscles would turn to mush. She'd be so stiff, she'd never be able to dance again. It was even worse than she'd imagined. She slammed the book shut and put it back on its shelf.

Patty had an appointment to see the orthopedic specialist on Friday afternoon. Her parents had told her not to be nervous. They would simply listen to what the doctor said, and then make their decision later.

I already know my decision, Patty thought, walking out of the library. *I am absolutely not going to wear that brace!*

* * *

"No, no," Madame Baril cried. "Patty, what are you thinking?"

If you only knew, Patty thought grimly. All she'd been able to think about through the whole class was that terrible brace she'd seen.

"Your expression must be like this." Madame Baril demonstrated how she wanted Patty to look while she danced the sequence. "Instead, you look like a miserable swan, as if you have no energy at all."

Kerry gave Patty a sympathetic look. It was the third rehearsal in a row in which Patty hadn't danced well. Kerry kept saying that Madame was being too hard, but Patty knew that she deserved the teacher's criticism. She'd been so nervous that nothing was coming out right—she was messing up moves she'd been able to do perfectly since she was eight years old.

She struggled through the rest of rehearsal, Madame correcting her at almost every turn. By the end of the hour she was fighting to hold back tears of frustration. She had never danced so poorly.

Finally Madame clapped her hands together, signaling the end of class. "Before you leave today, I would like to talk to all of you," she said. "Sit down, please."

All of the girls sat down in a circle around Madame Baril in the center of the studio. Patty suddenly realized she was sitting with her back to the front mirror, where Madame could see it clearly.

She scooted around so that her back was facing the side wall.

"I have made a decision," Madame Baril said slowly. "This was not easy for me, but I felt I had to do it." She paused for a minute, and Patty's mind raced.

"I am making a change in the casting. I have decided to give the role of Odette to Kerry."

Patty's jaw dropped. She felt as if Madame had just punched her in the stomach. This might be her last chance to perform, and Madame was taking it away from her!

Madame Baril looked at Patty. "Our rehearsals have not gone well, and I fear that Patty will not be ready by next week," she continued. "We all have so much work to do and so little time."

Patty felt everyone staring at her, but nobody said a word. They were all too shocked to speak.

"Patty, I think perhaps you are not ready for this role right now. Someday I know you will be," Madame Baril said. "All right, that's all for today. Next time we—"

"Wait," Kerry interrupted. "I want to say something."

Madame Baril turned to her. "What is it?"

"I think you should give Patty another chance," Kerry said.

Patty stared at Kerry in surprise.

"Kerry, I have made my decision," Madame Baril said firmly.

"But Patty's the best dancer for the role," Kerry insisted. "She's the most dramatic of all of us—and she's much stronger than I am. I think she should be the Swan Queen."

"You do, do you?" Madame Baril frowned. "I agree that Patty earned this part with her audition, but lately she has not been up to form. I am not sure why."

"I am," Kerry said.

Patty blinked in surprise. What was Kerry talking about? Nobody knew her secret!

"She's been having trouble concentrating on her jumps," Kerry said. "I think if we just work on those, everything will fall into place."

"We?" Madame Baril asked.

"Well, if it's OK with Patty, maybe she and I could stay late for the next few days and work on her jumps," Kerry said. "I'll try to help her."

Madame Baril looked at Kerry, and then at Patty. "All right, Kerry. If you think you can help Patty, you are welcome to try. But I can only give you two days. By Saturday, I need to see some improvement. In the meantime, Kerry, I'd like you to focus on learning the role, too."

Kerry nodded. "OK. Thanks, Madame. You won't regret this. I know Patty's going to be the perfect Odette."

"I hope so." Madame sighed and stood up. "All right, see you tomorrow, everyone."

Patty walked to the changing room in a daze.

She had almost lost the part to Kerry—and Kerry had been the one who'd gotten it back for her! She didn't understand. She would have thought Kerry would be thrilled to win the leading role. If she were Kerry, she would have taken it gladly. *Maybe Kerry's not like me*, she thought, opening her locker.

"I hope you don't mind what I did," Kerry said, coming over to her. "I really do think you deserve the part."

"No, it's OK," Patty said. "I mean, thank you."

"No problem," Kerry said. "I can't stay late today, but we could do it tomorrow. Is that OK?"

"Sure," Patty said. Having another girl stick up for her was a strange feeling—but a nice one. *I just hope I can prove Kerry right*, she thought.

Eight

◇

"So, how many people do we have now?" Mandy asked Jessica on Friday morning. They were standing in the hallway waiting for the final bell to ring.

"Ninety-seven," Jessica said. "I counted during the Hairnet's lecture to keep myself awake."

"Uh oh," Mandy said. "That gives us only a week to come up with another hundred people."

"Tell me about it," Jessica said. "I don't get it. Doesn't everyone want to be on TV?" She stopped a boy who was walking past them. "Did you hear about the dance marathon?"

"I've got a piano recital that day," he said. "Can't make it."

"But did you hear that it's going to be on TV?" Jessica called after him.

He turned around. "Yeah, I heard, but I still can't be there."

"You don't have to come for the whole time, you know," Mandy said. "You could come after your recital."

"Sorry," the boy said, walking away down the hall.

Jessica threw up her hands. "I don't see what's so important about a stupid piano recital. Everyone has such lame excuses!"

"It's just one person, Jessica," Mandy said. She waved to Janet, who was coming toward them.

"How did it go last night?" Jessica asked.

"Well, I called practically everyone I know. My parents yelled at me for being on the phone so much—I thought they were going to ground me again," Janet said.

"And? What happened?" Jessica wanted to know.

Janet smiled. "I got twenty-seven people to promise they'll dance."

"That's great!" Jessica exclaimed. As she and Mandy headed for their next class, Jessica shook her head. "You know, Mandy, this thing might actually work."

Patty felt as if she had been waiting forever. First she'd sat in the waiting room with her parents for ten minutes. Then the nurse had taken her into the X-ray room and she'd been in there for a while.

Now she was sitting on the edge of a blue plastic chair in one of the doctor's examining rooms, dressed in a thin cotton gown, waiting for him to come in.

Patty's parents had told her that this office was part of a big center where all kinds of problems were treated. In the waiting room outside Patty had seen an older man on crutches, a big guy who looked like a football player with a huge cast around his knee, and a little girl wearing an arm cast with stripes painted on it.

A tall man wearing a white doctor's coat opened the door and came in. "Hello there, Patty. I'm Dr. Maxwell." He held his hand out to her.

Patty shook it. She was embarrassed because her palms were damp from nervousness. "Hi," she said shyly.

"I'm sorry you had to wait. The lab was developing your X-rays." Dr. Maxwell smiled and held up a brown envelope he'd been carrying. He opened it and pulled out several large X-ray pictures. Then he stuck them onto a screen on one wall, and flicked a switch that made a light go on underneath the screen.

Patty cringed when she saw the X-ray. She didn't need the doctor to explain it to her. Up at the top, her spine made a big curve to the left, then further down her back it curved again, this time to the right. Looking at the huge curve on the X-ray, Patty couldn't believe everyone at school hadn't noticed it. Even more, she couldn't believe *she* hadn't noticed it!

"Patty, you have what is called an S-curve," Dr. Maxwell explained. "Actually, it's a backward S. See how the curve starts up here, on the left side? Then it goes back to the center, and over to the right. But before I go any further, let me get your parents." He pressed a button on his telephone. "Chris, please send in the Gilberts."

Patty sank down in her chair. This sounded serious.

"Dr. Ringwald tells me you're a dancer," Dr. Maxwell said while they waited. "How long have you been doing that?"

"Five years," Patty said. *And I don't want to quit*, she wanted to add.

"My daughter takes ballet lessons," Dr. Maxwell said. "She's just a beginner, but she loves it."

Mr. and Mrs. Gilbert walked into the office, looking very nervous. They sat down next to Patty.

"Is that her spine?" asked Mr. Gilbert, pointing to the X-ray.

"Yes, it is," Dr. Maxwell said. "I was just telling Patty that she has an S-curve. S-curves are difficult to detect, in case you're wondering why you hadn't noticed this. It's only noticeable if she bends over. Patty, would you show them, please?"

"Sure," Patty mumbled. She bit her lip and stood up.

"Now, pretend you're going to dive into a

pool," Dr. Maxwell said. Patty bent over. "See how her rib cage rotates slightly? And one of her shoulder blades is higher than the other, too."

No wonder Madame Baril noticed! Patty thought, straightening up and taking her seat.

"She has what is called a double major curve," Dr. Maxwell said. "That doesn't mean it's *more* major than another curve, or more serious—only that there is a major curve in both directions. She has a thirty-five degree curve."

"Is that serious?" asked Mrs. Gilbert.

"Anything over twenty is serious," the doctor said, "especially at Patty's age, when she's growing so fast."

"Will it keep growing that way?" Mr. Gilbert asked.

"Most likely it will," Dr. Maxwell said. "That's why I'm going to recommend that we treat it right away. Given Patty's age, and the fact that she's just grown a lot, I think we should catch this thing before it goes any further."

"How do we do that?" Mrs. Gilbert asked.

"My strong recommendation is that we get Patty fitted for the Milwaukee brace," Dr. Maxwell said.

"No!" Patty cried, jumping to her feet. "No! I won't wear that thing!"

"Honey, you don't even know what it is," Mr. Gilbert said, standing up and putting his arm around her shoulders.

"Yes, I do!" Patty said angrily, twisting away. "I looked it up! It's a big, huge, horrible thing, and I won't be able to dance ever again!"

"Patty, I know this is scary," Dr. Maxwell said soothingly. "I'm not going to do anything today except explain why I think this is the best thing to do. I think that once you consider the alternatives, you'll see that it isn't so bad. Lots of kids wear Milwaukee braces. They learn to live with them, and you can, too."

"But . . . you don't understand," Patty's mother said, her voice shaking. "Patty is a ballet dancer."

Dr. Maxwell nodded. "I realize that. Trust me —every girl I've treated for scoliosis has had to give up something temporarily. But Patty, I have some good news for you. We actually encourage patients to exercise while they're wearing the brace."

"Dance in a brace? How could I?" asked Patty, sinking back down onto her chair.

"Once you get used to it, you'll be able to do practically everything in it. Also, we may be able to allow you to take it off occasionally for ballet. Not every day, of course, but now and then."

"Are you saying she has to wear this brace twenty-four hours a day?" asked Mrs. Gilbert. "How will she shower? Get dressed? How will she sleep?"

"She can remove the brace to take a shower. But basically, we require patients to wear it twenty-three hours a day. We've found that it simply works best that way. I could see letting Patty remove it three days a week to dance for an hour. Ballet exercises seem to be good for the recovery process, as is swimming," Dr. Maxwell explained. He gave Patty a searching look. "How do you feel about all this, now that I've explained it a little more?"

Patty had been scratching her nails against the plastic seat. She didn't know what to say. What was there to say? "What about an operation? You could just fix it and then I wouldn't have to give up dancing at all."

Dr. Maxwell shook his head, looking serious. "Well, surgery is an option. But for your type of curve, I wouldn't recommend it. There's always a risk when you go into the operating room. You'll avoid that with the brace."

"I don't want Patty to have an operation," Mrs. Gilbert said firmly. Mr. Gilbert nodded.

"Isn't there another kind of brace, one that isn't so big?" Patty asked.

"There is something called the Boston brace," Dr. Maxwell said. "Those are premade to fit a variety of shapes and sizes. It's not as big as a Milwaukee, but sometimes it's not as effective, either. The advantage to the Milwaukee is that it's fitted exactly to your body. We take a mold of you and the brace is built specifically for you. Patty, if you want to straighten this curve quickly so you can get back to your dancing, I'd have to recommend the Milwaukee."

"How long will all this take?" asked Mr. Gilbert.

Dr. Maxwell tapped his fingers against the desk. "At least two years. It's hard to say exactly, though—it might be only two years, or it might be three or four."

Patty felt as if she was going to faint. At least *two years*? By the time she got the brace off, she'd be in high school!

"The reason it's important to start soon is that Patty's still growing, and her spine is not mature yet. We have a terrific chance of catching this thing, but we'll want to start as soon as possible, before Patty's body matures any further."

A dull silence fell over the room. Patty was too stunned to move. Her whole life seemed to be crashing down around her. She knew that if she lost two years of practice now she'd never be a premiere dancer, no matter how hard she tried to catch up later.

"Why don't you get changed, Patty," Dr. Maxwell said. "I need to talk to your parents about a few things."

Patty got up and wandered into the bathroom attached to Dr. Maxwell's office, where she'd left her clothes. She glanced at her reflection in the mirror as she pulled on her sweatshirt. It was a souvenir from a trip to San Francisco, where she'd gone to see a famous ballet company from Russia. "To dance is to fly!" it said in big pink letters.

Patty took off the sweatshirt, turned it inside out, and then put it back on.

Nine

◇

"That was much better today," Madame Baril told Patty after rehearsal later that afternoon. "You danced as if you were inspired. I think perhaps Kerry was right about giving you another chance." She smiled at Patty.

Patty felt as if her heart was going to break in half. If only Madame knew why she was so inspired! But she couldn't tell her. She wasn't going to tell anyone until after the performance. "Thanks," she said. "I'll try to keep it up."

"Don't work too long, girls," Madame called to Patty and Kerry as she left the studio. "I don't want you to be overtired."

"Madame was right," Kerry said once their

teacher was gone. "You seemed like the old Patty today."

Patty smiled. For the first time since *Swan Lake* rehearsals had started she had been able to put her worries out of her mind. *There's nothing wrong with me*, she kept thinking, *and there's no reason I can't be a perfect Odette for Madame Baril.*

"So what do you want to work on first?" Kerry asked.

"Well, what do you think I should work on?" Patty asked.

"I guess we could start with the opening sequence of the act," Kerry said. "I'll look for any problems I think you're having, then we can focus on them."

"You sound just like Madame," Patty said with a laugh, heading for the corner of the studio so she could make her entrance.

"Only I'm a lot nicer, right?" Kerry called over to her.

"Right," Patty replied. Kerry *was* very nice.

Kerry put the tape of *Swan Lake* into the cassette player mounted in the wall and fast-forwarded it to the right spot. "Ready?" she called to Patty.

"I'm ready," Patty replied. She took a deep breath. As soon as Kerry started the tape, Patty's body sprang into action. She had memorized the steps so perfectly that she simply shut off her brain and let her body feel the music. She remembered what Madame Baril had told her—she was supposed to be longing, and yet afraid, mirroring the sound of Tchaikovsky's music. For the first time since the audition, Patty knew she was truly dancing, the way she had always dreamed of doing.

Only when the music ended did Patty remember that Kerry was in the room, watching her. "How was I?" she asked nervously, walking over to her.

"Fantastic," Kerry said. "The only problem I can see is in some of your jumps, like I told Madame. If you get those right, you're going to be absolutely amazing."

"Really?" Patty felt pleased by Kerry's compliment.

Kerry nodded. "Really." She stepped out to the center of the floor. "OK, this is what you want to do, right?" She leaped into the air, demonstrating the small jump.

Patty shook her head. "You make it look so easy!"

"You know what? I think you should forget all about your role for a few minutes," Kerry said. "Maybe you've been trying too hard to get everything perfect, and that's why it's not working." She walked over to the edge of the studio. "You know the opening sequence the rest of us are doing, right?"

Patty nodded. She'd studied *Swan Lake* often enough to know most of the parts.

"You know how we come on stage with a *jeté*, and then do those high prancing steps, like this?" Kerry leaped from one foot to the other. "You try it. Get as much height as you can. Then maybe when you go back to your steps, they'll be fresher and you can put more into them."

"That's a good idea. One of my old ballet teachers used to have us switch roles a lot," Patty said. "That way if anyone got sick there was someone who knew the part. Once I had to fill in at the last minute for this girl who came down with the chicken pox the day of the recital."

"Wow, that must have been scary," Kerry said.

"Not really," Patty said, walking over to the side of the studio to make her entrance. "It was almost fun, because I didn't even have time to worry about it—I just had to do it." Thinking back on the experience made Patty smile. That was when she had first realized that maybe she did have something special. She knew that not everyone could have jumped in at the last minute like that.

"OK, let's see it," Kerry said.

Patty did a small *jeté* with one leg in a low *arabesque*, then started prancing across the studio, kicking her legs out to the front. As she pranced, she jumped as high as she could.

"Looking good," Kerry yelled.

Patty knew she was moving very well—and she was having fun, too. What a change from her rehearsals lately!

"That was fun," she said when she came to a stop. "I feel like doing it again!"

Kerry laughed. "OK, but let's do it together. We won't make up a whole *corps* of swans, but at least we'll be two." She and Patty strode over to the corner of the studio.

"Wait—let's put on the music, too," Patty said. She ran over and found the right spot on the tape, at the beginning of the second act of the ballet. "Ready?" Kerry nodded, and Patty started the tape. Then she ran over and stood next to Kerry.

They started with the *jeté*. Patty caught their reflection in the mirror, their bodies moving in complete coordination. They did look like swans in Patty's eyes.

"Let's do it again," said Kerry breathlessly when they had finished. "This time let's see how high we can jump."

"OK," Patty agreed. If she was going to have to quit dancing, at least she was going to go out in style.

She and Kerry took a few extra steps before they sprang into the air. When Patty leaped up into the air, she glanced in the mirror again. She saw herself dancing gracefully, getting excellent elevation.

But as she continued to prance, a terrible picture invaded her mind. She saw herself trying to jump while wearing a brace over her leotard. She could see the metal holding her like a cage, so tight and constricting she couldn't even move.

Patty was so shocked by the image that she landed incorrectly, and her legs crumpled beneath her. She fell, her elbows slamming against the hard-wood floor.

"Patty! Are you all right?" Kerry stopped dancing and rushed to her side.

Patty felt as if something inside her had been jarred loose. But it wasn't a bone, or a joint, or her back. It was everything she'd been holding inside for so long—everything she'd been trying to hide from everyone, including herself.

In that moment, crouched on the floor, she knew she wasn't going to become a dancer, not in the way she wanted to be. She'd never dance *Swan Lake* in front of a huge crowd, or travel around the world as a ballerina, or even make it into the *corps* of some small dance company. She wasn't ever going to be anything but plain old Patty Gilbert, stuck in a brace.

"Patty?" Kerry asked, looking worried. "Are you OK? Say something!" She bent over next to Patty just as a tear ran down Patty's cheek. "Oh, no —you're hurt, aren't you? It's all my fault. We shouldn't have been doing all those jumps!"

Patty shook her head, as the tears started to flow more freely. "It's not . . . your fault," she choked out. Then she got to her feet and ran out of the studio.

*   *   *

Kerry sat down on the edge of the stage next to Patty and touched her arm. "I've been looking all over for you. Are you OK? Does anything hurt?" she asked gently.

Patty shook her head and wiped the tears off her face. She'd been crying uncontrollably for the past several minutes. She had hidden on the dark stage, hoping that Kerry would give up on her and leave the studio.

"Then what is it?" Kerry asked.

"I—I have something wrong with my back," Patty said. She was surprised to find herself confiding in Kerry. But she'd been so nice, and Patty felt as if she had to tell someone. "I have to start wearing a brace."

"What?" Kerry looked shocked. "What's wrong with your back?"

"It's called scoliosis," Patty explained. Just saying the word out loud made her feel strangely relieved. "It means that my spine is curved instead of straight. The doctor says I have to get it straightened or it's going to get worse."

Kerry didn't say anything for a minute. "And that's why you need to wear this brace—to straighten it?" she finally asked.

Patty nodded, swinging her legs back and forth off the edge of the stage. "I have to wear it for two years. Can you believe it? I'm not going to be able to dance at all."

"Really?" Kerry's lip trembled, and she looked as if she were going to start crying, too. "Patty, that's terrible."

"Yeah. The doctor said I could still take class maybe three times a week," Patty told Kerry. "I have to wear the brace as much as possible, though."

Kerry's eyes lit up. "That's good. So you could still dance!"

"But it's not going to be the same."

"I know," Kerry said. "I mean, I don't know, exactly, but I can imagine." She looked at Patty thoughtfully. "How did all this happen?"

Patty shrugged. "The doctor said they don't know why it happens."

"It doesn't seem fair," Kerry said.

"I know." Patty looked down at her hands. "I'll never be a great dancer now. Even if the doctor lets me dance an hour a day, by the time I get my brace off it'll be too late."

"Maybe not," Kerry said. "I've heard of famous dancers who didn't really get started until they were fourteen or fifteen."

"Really?"

"Sure," Kerry said. "So when do you have to get your brace?" She gasped and put her hand over her mouth. "It isn't before the performance, is it? Is *that* why you've been so nervous?"

"N-no," Patty said. "I was so nervous because Madame's the one who noticed something was a little weird about my posture, and she kept harping on it. I haven't told her the truth yet."

"I wonder what she's going to say," Kerry said. "I bet she'll be really nice about it."

Patty looked up. "You think so?"

Kerry nodded. "You know, if I were you, I'd get that brace on right away. Because the sooner you get it on, the sooner you'll get it off."

Patty hadn't thought about it that way. She'd wanted to delay putting that brace on as long as possible—preferably forever. But Kerry had a point. "Maybe I will."

"But definitely wait until after our performance," Kerry said. "It wouldn't be fair if you had to give up your starring role. Besides, it's only one week away now."

Patty hugged her knees to her chest. "I don't know what to do. Ever since I found out something was wrong with my back, I've been dancing terribly. Maybe it would be better if I just gave the role to you. After all, if I tell Madame the truth, she may not want me to dance." She sighed. "The doctor said it was OK for me to keep dancing, but I don't know. I'm not sure I can go through with it."

Kerry was silent for a moment. "I'm not sure what you should do," she said at last. "But whenever I have to make a decision, I always head straight to Casey's for a sundae. I think that's what you need right now."

Patty smiled. "You think so?"

Kerry nodded. "Definitely. My treat."

"I don't know," Patty said. "I should probably get home. My parents might be worried about me."

"Call them," Kerry said.

Patty hesitated. "Well, OK," she said finally. "I haven't had a sundae in a long time."

"I know ballerinas aren't supposed to eat banana splits, but I think I'm going to make an exception today," Kerry said with a mischievous grin.

"Maybe we could split a split," Patty suggested.

Kerry laughed. "It's a deal!"

Ten

◇

"I've wanted to be a ballerina since I was six," Kerry told Patty as they walked into the mall. "My dad wanted me to play baseball, though. It took a long time to convince him to let me take lessons."

"So how long have you been dancing?" asked Patty. Ever since they left the dance studio, the two girls had been talking nonstop—about dancing, school, friends, family, and everything else they could think of.

"Three years," Kerry said.

"Wow, only three years and you're already really good," Patty said, impressed. "I've been taking ballet since I was seven."

"Do you think about it all the time?" Kerry asked. "I do. Sometimes I'm sitting in class and I'm supposed to be paying attention to some filmstrip or something, and all I can picture is myself dancing the opening steps of some ballet."

Patty giggled. "Me, too."

"Look, a bunch of my friends are here," Kerry said when they entered Casey's. She pointed at a table near the back. Patty recognized Jessica Wakefield and several of the other members of the Unicorn Club.

"Hey, Kerry," Belinda Layton said. "Have a seat, you guys." She moved her chair over so that they could squeeze in two extra chairs.

"You guys all know Patty, right?" Kerry asked.

"Hi," everyone at the table said.

"Hi," Patty said shyly, sitting down next to Kerry.

The waitress stopped at their table and Kerry ordered a banana split. She gave Patty a mischievous smile, and Patty couldn't help smiling back.

"So how's *Swan Lake* going?" Jessica asked.

"Pretty well," Kerry said. "I can tell the performance is getting close, though. I'm starting to get nervous!"

"If you're nervous, Patty must be a wreck," Mandy Miller exclaimed. She turned to Patty. "You have the lead, right?"

Patty nodded, looking down at her hands.

"I heard Madame Baril is a real workhorse," Jessica said. "At least that's what Kerry always says."

Kerry rolled her eyes dramatically, and everybody laughed.

"She is pretty tough," Patty admitted. "But she's the best teacher I've ever had. I'm going to miss her," she added, almost to herself.

"Why? Are you moving away?" Mary Wallace asked.

Patty looked up in surprise. "Oh, no. I just . . ." She looked over at Kerry, who smiled reassuringly. "I just found out I have scoliosis." Patty took a deep breath. If she'd been surprised to find herself confiding in Kerry earlier, she was doubly surprised to find herself confiding in this whole group of girls she barely knew. She'd always been a little bit intimidated by the Unicorns, but now that she was sitting here talking to them, they really seemed nice. "It means that something's wrong with my back, and I'm going to have to wear a brace for a while."

"Wow," Jessica said. "That's a real bummer."

"You know what?" Mandy said. "When I was in the hospital, I had this really nice volunteer who told me she had scoliosis. She was in high school. She had just gotten her brace off, and she was super excited."

"What does the brace do?" Mary asked.

"My spine is curved, and it will help to straighten it," Patty said.

"Really? It's curved? But you don't look like it. I mean, your posture's really perfect," Jessica said.

She grinned. "And after going to charm school, we all know how important good posture is."

Patty smiled. She, Jessica, and some of the other girls had recently attended a charm school that had opened in Sweet Valley. But Jessica's twin sister, Elizabeth, and two of her friends had discovered that the school was a front for a group of burglars. "It's OK now," Patty explained. "But if I don't wear the brace, I probably would start looking a little funny pretty soon."

"How did you get it?" Belinda asked. "I mean, is it something you were born with?"

"No, not really," Patty said. "They don't know what causes it yet." She turned to Mandy. "Why were you in the hospital?"

"I had cancer," Mandy said.

Patty was startled. "That's pretty serious," she said, not really knowing what else to say. She had never known anyone with cancer before, much less someone her own age. And here she was, feeling sorry for herself just because she had to wear a brace for a couple of years!

"Yeah, it was," Mandy said. "But I'm better now. Anyway, you could talk to this volunteer if you want to know what it's like to wear a brace. I think she had it on for two and a half years. She said it was hard at first, but after a while she hardly noticed it."

"There's a girl I used to play soccer against who wore a brace," Belinda said. "I never knew what it was for—she was on another team, so I only saw her a couple of times. But she was a great player."

"When do you think you'll get your brace?" asked Mary.

Patty shrugged. "In a couple of weeks, I guess. I have to get fitted for it first."

"So you can still dance in *Swan Lake*," Jessica said. "That's good. At least you won't miss out on your starring role."

"Yeah, I think I can still do it," Patty said, watching as the waitress set down the banana split in front of Kerry.

"You're going to," Kerry said, sliding the banana split toward Patty and handing her a spoon.

"You know what? If you're not getting your brace right away, you could dance in the dance marathon," Jessica said.

"Great idea!" Mandy exclaimed.

Mary groaned. "Give in now, Patty," she warned. "Otherwise Jessica and Mandy will pester you to death."

Patty laughed. "All right then, I surrender. It sounds like fun."

"Terrific!" Mandy said. She consulted a sheet of paper on the table. "That makes one hundred and forty-seven people, including you. Look out, Big Mesa!"

"There's just one little thing they're not telling you, Patty," Belinda commented dryly. "This marathon of theirs starts next Saturday at ten in the morning, and lasts until nine-thirty at night."

"Hey, stop complaining, Belinda," Jessica said, shaking a finger at her jokingly. "I thought you were supposed to be an athlete."

Patty smiled even wider as she watched the others joking around. She couldn't remember the last time she'd felt this good. She'd forgotten how nice it was just to hang out with friends and have fun.

"Give me your phone number," Mandy said to Patty. "I'll call you this weekend and give you all the details, OK?"

As Patty jotted down her number on a napkin, she couldn't help thinking how ironic it was that it had taken the horrible news about her brace to show her how important friends can be.

"Mom told me you hung out with some friends last night," Jana said when she came down to breakfast on Saturday morning. "Did you have fun?"

Patty smiled. "Uh huh. We ate ice cream and then walked around the mall for a while."

Jana got a glass of orange juice and sat down at the kitchen table. "Mom and Dad also told me what the doctor said yesterday." She looked into Patty's eyes. "I'm sorry I got home too late last night to talk to you about it. How are you doing?"

Patty shrugged. "OK, I guess."

"OK? Patty, you're amazing." Jana shook her head. "If I were you, I'd be going nuts!"

"I didn't mean I was *excited* about it," Patty said, rolling her eyes.

Jana laughed. "Well, how do you feel?"

"At first I thought I was going to go crazy," Patty said. "I really did. I couldn't imagine ever having to wear a brace or have surgery or anything. And I couldn't stand the thought that I was going to have to stop dancing. But after I told Kerry about it, I didn't feel so bad."

"Who's Kerry?" asked Jana. "Wait a sec—isn't she that girl in your dance class who you don't like?"

Patty smiled. "No, I like her. She's—my friend, I guess. We were rehearsing yesterday and everything kind of got to me. She was really understanding." Patty paused for a minute. "I think I felt so rotten because I felt like I had to deal with the whole thing on my own. I didn't want anyone in dance class to know because I was afraid I'd lose my solo in the performance."

"I can understand that," Jana said. "But now you're not worried about that anymore?"

"Well, I guess I still am, a little. But once I told her I felt so . . . relieved, I guess," Patty said.

"Yeah, whenever I'm upset about something, I feel better the second I tell a friend."

Patty nodded. Friends were something Jana

had always had to rely on. But Patty had been a loner ever since she'd gotten serious about ballet.

The phone rang, and Jana got up to answer it. "Hello? Yes, I think so. Who's calling? OK, I'll check." She put the phone down on the table. "Are Mom and Dad here?"

"They're outside, working in the yard," Patty said.

"It's Dr. Maxwell," Jana told her, going to the door to call their parents.

Patty felt her stomach tighten. She hoped he didn't have more bad news. Doctors didn't usually work on Saturdays, did they?

Mr. Gilbert hurried into the kitchen and picked up the phone. Patty listened nervously to her father's end of the conversation. "Yes, Doctor. Mm hmm. Yes, I understand. Well, that is an opportunity. I see. We'll talk to Patty about it, and I'll give you a call back. This morning? OK, then. We'll talk about it right away. Thank you." He hung up.

Mrs. Gilbert came in the door, pulling off her gardening gloves. "What did Dr. Maxwell want?"

Mr. Gilbert sat down at the kitchen table. "He was calling about having Patty fitted for a brace right away." He turned to Patty. "Do you feel ready to go ahead with this?"

Patty nodded. "I guess if I have to get my back fixed, it's the best way. That's what Dr. Maxwell said."

Mrs. Gilbert came over and put her arm

around Patty's shoulders. "Patty, sweetheart, we're so proud of you, do you know that?"

"I'm not going to enjoy this or anything, but at least I'll get better," Patty said.

"Dr. Maxwell was calling because they've had a sudden opening down at the clinic," Mr. Gilbert explained. "The orthotist—that's the specialist who makes the braces—could do the mold for your brace next Friday."

"But Friday is the day of the performance," Mrs. Gilbert said.

"I know," Patty's father said. "But the appointment's at two, so she'd be done in plenty of time. He said if we don't grab this spot, it might be weeks before we can get another."

Patty thought about it for a minute. If she had to have a brace, maybe Kerry was right. The sooner she got it on, the sooner it would come off.

"Well? What should I tell Dr. Maxwell?" Mr. Gilbert asked. "Do you want to wait a little longer, Patty? It's up to you."

Patty shook her head. "No. Tell him Friday is fine."

The truth was, there was something she was dreading even more than getting the brace—and that was telling Madame Baril the truth.

"Patty, why aren't you dressed?" Madame Baril asked when Patty walked into the studio five minutes after rehearsal was supposed to begin Monday afternoon.

She had been stalling outside, walking back and forth outside the dance studio, trying to get up her nerve.

Patty swallowed. "I need to talk to you—to everyone," she said.

"About what?" asked Madame Baril. "We don't have much time, as you know. There is still much to be done if we are to be ready for our performance."

"This won't take long," Patty said. "I just wanted to tell you that you were right—there is something wrong with me. I have scoliosis. And if you don't want me to dance next week, I'll understand."

Madame Baril looked at her in surprise. "But you told me—"

"I lied," said Patty. "I'm sorry, Madame Baril. I was afraid if I went to the doctor and found out something was wrong, I wouldn't be able to dance in *Swan Lake*. I wanted that role more than anything. Then when I did go, and the doctor told me I had it, I still didn't want to give up dancing in the performance."

"Oh, Patty, I'm so sorry," Jo said. She walked over and gave Patty's arm a little squeeze.

"If I am not mistaken," Madame Baril said, "there is nothing wrong with dancing while you have scoliosis. So why can't you dance next week?"

"I can, if you still want me to," Patty said. "I just thought maybe . . ."

"Nonsense," Madame Baril said. "When will you get your brace?"

"In a few weeks. I'll be fitted for it on Friday," Patty said.

Madame Baril nodded. "I see. Did your doctor say you could continue to dance—with the brace, I mean?"

"Yes, probably. He said I could take it off and dance for an hour a few times a week," Patty said.

"Good." Madame Baril nodded. "Well, until then, are you allowed to dance full-time?"

"Yes," Patty said nervously.

"Then I expect to see you back here dressed for class in five minutes," Madame said sternly. And then, Patty was almost sure, she saw Madame smile.

Eleven

"Hello, Jessica. This is Brian, Hollywood Jones's assistant."

Jessica's heart leaped. "Hello," she said, trying her best to sound mature and organized. *It's a good thing I came right home after school today*, she thought.

"I'm calling to give you an update on our visit," Brian said.

Jessica gasped. "You're still coming, aren't you?"

"Yes, of course. I just wanted to let you know we'll swing by your school early Friday to interview you and anyone else involved with the marathon," Brian said.

"Interview me? On TV? Oh, sure, of course,"

Jessica said. She couldn't believe it! Hollywood Jones was going to interview *her*!

"And we'll plan to come by a few times on Saturday to catch the beginning, middle, and end of the marathon," Brian said. "How does that sound?"

"Sounds great to me," Jessica said.

"OK then, we'll be seeing you," Brian said cheerfully.

Jessica hung up the phone. She was staring dreamily into space when Elizabeth walked in the door.

"Jessica, are you all right?" Elizabeth asked, setting her backpack on a kitchen chair. "You don't look so good."

Jessica grabbed her twin's arms and started dancing her around in a circle. "I'm really going to be on TV!"

"Did you talk to *Hollywood* again?" Elizabeth teased her.

"No, but I'm going to—he's going to interview me on Friday!" She couldn't wait until everyone at school heard about this.

"Do you want something to drink?" Patty asked Kerry. "My dad said dinner will be ready in about half an hour."

"No, thanks. I want to see your room, though," Kerry said.

"OK." Patty led her upstairs. It had been a

long time since she'd had a friend over. In fact, this was the first time since her family had moved to Sweet Valley.

"This is really nice," Kerry said when Patty opened the door to her room. "What a cool poster." She pointed to a poster of a dancer doing an *arabesque*. She walked over to get a closer look at some of the pictures of famous ballerinas on the walls.

"Thanks," Patty said, sitting down on her bed. "Do you have a lot of ballet stuff in your room, too?"

Kerry nodded. "Yeah, I have so much junk on the walls, it drives my mom crazy. It's not only ballet, though. I have a bunch of pictures of Johnny Buck, too."

Patty leaned back on her bed. "Now that I won't be spending so much time dancing, maybe I'll get into music, too."

Kerry sat down beside her. "I can loan you some tapes, if you want." She smoothed Patty's bedspread. "Are you worried about getting your brace mold done?"

"A little. Dr. Maxwell told me how they're going to do it, so at least I know what to expect." Patty leaned back and stared at the ceiling. "First they wrap me in a frame so that I stay straight, and they use some kind of strap to align my hips and waist. Then they dunk strips of gauze into plaster and put them all over the top of my body. When it dries, they take it off and use the shape to make the brace.''

"It sounds like papier mâché," Kerry said.

"That's exactly what I said." Patty laughed. "I'd much rather have a costume fitting."

"You're really brave, Patty. I don't know if I could go through with that," Kerry said.

Patty sat up and shrugged. "It's because I have to, I guess."

"You know, if you . . . if you think you'll need some moral support or something," Kerry began, plucking at the bedspread with her fingers, "I don't think I'm doing anything Friday afternoon . . ."

"Would you come with me?" Patty asked.

Kerry laughed. "That's what I was trying to say."

"Thanks, Kerry." Patty smiled at her new friend. "That would be great."

"Do I look OK?" Jessica asked her sister, glancing into the rearview mirror of the television station's on-location van and smoothing back her hair. It was Friday morning, and Jessica was waiting for her interview with Hollywood Jones to begin.

"For the fifteenth time, you look great," Elizabeth said, rolling her eyes.

Jessica smiled. "Thanks." She glanced over to where Hollywood Jones was standing, surrounded by a hairstylist, a makeup person, and several other members of the crew. "Speaking of looking great, Hollywood Jones is even better-looking in person than he is on the show."

"All right, girls," the assistant producer called out. "We're ready for you."

Jessica hurried over to the school steps, where Mandy was already waiting. Even though it was still early, a large group of kids was gathered on the sides of the steps and down on the lawn to watch. Hollywood strode over to a spot right in front of the camera. He was wearing a blue linen blazer, a white T-shirt, and sunglasses.

"I'm so nervous," Mandy said out of the corner of her mouth. Jessica took a deep breath and flashed Hollywood her brightest smile. But he was already grinning engagingly at the camera.

"Hello everyone, and welcome to . . ." Hollywood said. He paused and looked around expectantly.

"Sweet Valley!" everyone yelled at the top of their lungs, just as they'd been told to do.

"Fooled you, didn't we?" Hollywood winked at the camera. "We're here to watch a dance marathon, one that the kids promise me is going to shatter the existing record into a million pieces." He took a few steps backward and shoved the microphone in Jessica's face. "Tell us about it."

Jessica gulped. "Hi there, I'm Jessica Wakefield. Um, we're trying to break the record for dancing the longest. Tomorrow, we're going to dance for eleven and a half hours."

"Wow!" Hollywood wiped his forehead and pretended to look exhausted. "How will you last?" He pointed the mike at Mandy this time.

"We've been practicing," Mandy said. "And we're going to have lots of food—we got a restaurant to donate snacks. Plus, people are really excited about this, so there's a lot of energy in the air."

"Now, this is the state record for kids under fourteen, right?" Hollywood said.

"That's right," Jessica said. "We wanted to break a longer record, but we'd have to skip school to do that."

Hollywood nodded. "Very interesting. All right, tell us about your school. Is this the kind of project everyone gets involved in?"

Jessica smiled. "Totally," she said smoothly. "Everyone's behind it one-hundred percent. We're really excited."

Mandy shot Jessica a look. "Of course, not everyone could participate because of other things they have to do," she explained. "Like sports practices and—"

"What's going on?" a tall, pretty girl with shoulder-length, silky dark hair interrupted, walking up the steps toward them. Jessica had never seen her before. "Hey, you're Hollywood Jones," the girl said.

"And are you one of the dancers in the marathon?" Hollywood asked, smiling at her.

"What marathon?" she asked.

"Uh, she doesn't go to school here, that's why she doesn't know about it," Jessica explained quickly.

"I do so go to school here," the girl said. "Is there a dance marathon? Oh, I get it—it'll be on your show."

Hollywood nodded. "Do you think we'll see you out there?"

"Oh, definitely," she said, with a big smile. "I love to dance."

"OK, then, we'll see you on the dance floor," Hollywood said. He turned to the camera. "Stay tuned for the dance marathon of the year, coming straight to you from Sweet Valley! Everyone remember to take your vitamins tomorrow morning!" he yelled to the crowd.

"It's a wrap," the assistant producer said. "Let's get to our next stop." Within minutes, the small crew had packed up their things.

Hollywood winked at Jessica. "Nice job. See you tomorrow." Then he ran down the steps and hopped into the van.

Jessica's friends came rushing over to her. "Great job, you guys," Mary exclaimed. "You were so calm!"

"It was OK except for that dumb girl who butted in front of the camera and made us look like idiots," Jessica said. She hated having the limelight stolen.

"Who was that girl?" Janet asked. "I've never seen her before."

"There she is," Ellen said. The girl was strolling toward them, looking bored.

"Hi," Janet said as the stranger approached. "What's your name?"

"Veronica Brooks," the girl replied, running a hand through her hair. "Why?"

"You said you go to school here?" Ellen asked.

"This is my first day," Veronica said. "And to tell you the truth, this place is pretty pathetic compared to my old school in Cedar Springs."

"So you just moved here?" Lila asked.

Veronica nodded. "Unfortunately, yeah. We just moved into this crummy house in a neighborhood full of geriatrics—oh, except for the people next door. There's this girl who sings Johnny Buck songs really loudly in her swimming pool. She has a terrible voice."

Everyone turned to stare at Lila, whose face was bright pink.

"Gee, I wonder who that could be?" Ellen said innocently.

"So you live in the big brick house on Highland Avenue?" Jessica asked Veronica.

"Yeah, how did you know that?"

Jessica smiled and turned to Lila. "Veronica, meet your new neighbor."

*   *   *

"Wow, this place is huge," Kerry said to Patty as they walked into the orthopedic center where Patty was going to have her mold made. Kerry had gotten out of school a little early so she could come along.

Patty nodded. She glanced over at Kerry shyly. "I'm really glad you could come with me. It's nice to have moral support."

Kerry smiled. "No problem."

Patty walked up to the reception desk. "Hi, I'm here to see the orthotist. My name's Patty Gilbert."

"Hello, Patty." The receptionist looked down at her appointment book. "Sandy's just finishing up with someone right now. Why don't you take a seat, and I'll tell her you're here."

"OK," Patty said. She and Kerry went and sat down in the waiting area near a large tank filled with colorful fish.

"Look," Kerry said. She pointed to a girl who had just come in and was heading for the reception desk.

"What?" asked Patty.

"She's wearing a brace," Kerry said. "See that thing around her neck?"

"Oh." Patty stared at the girl. She looked as if she was about fourteen or fifteen. She was very pretty, with long, wavy dark-brown hair. Patty had never seen a brace on a real, live person before. It didn't look nearly as bad as it had in the picture she had seen.

After speaking with the receptionist for a moment, the girl walked over and sat down on a couch a few yards away from Patty and Kerry.

"Let's talk to her," Kerry said. "You could ask her what wearing a brace will be like."

"I don't know. I don't want to bug her," Patty said hesitantly. She didn't think *she* would like it if a total stranger came up to her just to ask about her brace.

"Come on," Kerry said. "I bet she wouldn't mind."

"Well, OK." Patty got up and went over to the girl, with Kerry right behind her. "Hi," she said. "My name's Patty, and this is my friend Kerry."

The girl smiled at them. "I'm Theresa."

"I don't mean to bother you," Patty began, a little nervously, "but I found out recently that I have scoliosis, and I noticed you're wearing a brace. I'm being fitted for one this afternoon."

"You are?" Theresa smiled at Patty. "Don't worry. It's really not too bad. It takes forever, though."

"You have scoliosis too, right?" Kerry asked.

"Yeah, I developed it when I was eleven," Theresa said. "I've been wearing this brace for three years. I know what you must be thinking—three years! Oh, no!" She laughed. "But it hasn't been that bad. I mean, at first it was a real pain to get used to. But now I hardly notice it."

"Really?" Patty said.

"Uh huh. Who's your doctor?"

"Dr. Maxwell," Patty said.

"Mine, too," Theresa said. "He's great. When he first told me I had to get a brace, I wanted to kill him, but since then it's been OK."

"Do you come here to get the brace adjusted?" Patty asked Theresa.

"Yeah. I think I have about six more months to go. I just want to get it off before my junior year so I can join the gymnastics team. Dr. Maxwell says I'll definitely make that. I can't wait! The worst thing about getting this brace was having to stop doing gymnastics for a while."

"I take ballet," Patty said. "Dr. Maxwell said I can still do it a little, but not as much as I have been."

Theresa nodded sympathetically. "Dr. Maxwell said it wouldn't be a good idea for me to do any gymnastics at all, but he did say I should start swimming an hour a day. So I've been swimming for the last three years, and now, as soon as I get this brace off, I'm going out for the swim team, too. I love swimming almost as much as gymnastics now—it's kind of weird how things turn out, huh?"

Patty nodded. "I hope things turn out OK for me, too."

"I have a feeling they will," Theresa said with

a smile. "Here." She opened her purse and took out a small pad of paper and a pen. "Write down your name and phone number, and I'll give you mine. That way, if you have any questions, or if you want to talk, you can call me."

"OK." Patty jotted down her number, and then took the slip of paper Theresa handed her. "Thanks!"

"No problem." Theresa smiled.

"Thanks, Kerry," Patty said, after Theresa had been called into the doctor's office.

"For what?" Kerry asked.

"For getting me to talk to her. She's really amazing. If she can get through three years of that brace, so can I."

"You can do anything you want," Kerry said confidently.

Patty stared at the fish swimming gracefully around the tank. "I'm not so sure," she said quietly.

"What do you mean?"

Patty looked at Kerry seriously. "I'm not sure I can get through the performance tonight."

Twelve

◇

"I still can't decide what to wear tomorrow," Jessica said to Elizabeth on Friday night as they stood outside the dance studio, waiting for Patty's performance to begin.

"I thought you picked out your outfit last week," Elizabeth said. Sometimes she couldn't believe how much time Jessica spent thinking about clothes.

"I did, but that was before I knew I was going to be the star of the show." Jessica tapped her foot against the sidewalk. "I mean, after today, I'm pretty sure Hollywood's going to show lots of shots of me at the marathon."

"And the other hundred and fifty people who signed up," Elizabeth reminded her.

"Yeah, but I'm the one he interviewed. He knows me now," Jessica said confidently. "I bet he'll hang out with me all night."

Elizabeth laughed. "Come on. We should probably go inside now so we can get good seats."

As Elizabeth opened the door to the studio, she realized that her sister was still standing in the middle of the sidewalk, staring up at the sky.

"Hey, Jess, time to come back to earth," Elizabeth said, going over and tugging on her sleeve. "Even though I know you'd rather stare into space and think about Hollywood."

"He is pretty gorgeous," Jessica said. "But actually, I was just thinking about how brilliant I am. Do you realize that without me, this dance marathon wouldn't even be happening? And now it's going to be on TV, and—"

"Yeah, yeah, I know," Elizabeth said. "I have the smartest twin ever. There's only one problem. What if those hundred and fifty people don't show up tomorrow?"

"Oh, they'll show up," Jessica said with a wave of her hand. "Everyone wants to be on TV, right?"

Patty was standing in front of the mirror in the changing room, adjusting her costume for about the hundredth time. With shaking fingers she tucked a few stray wisps of hair back into her bun. She'd already applied and reapplied her lipstick several times to make sure it was perfect. She was so nervous she couldn't hold still.

She'd come to the studio an hour earlier than everyone else to go through the dance, hoping to iron out any remaining problems. She had had so much trouble since Madame had first mentioned seeing something strange about her posture that she was scared she wouldn't ever dance well again. And this was her last chance. Tonight, more than ever, she wanted to dance beautifully.

"Patty, you look wonderful."

In the mirror Patty saw Madame Baril walking up behind her. Madame made a small adjustment to Patty's headpiece. "I knew all along you were the right dancer for the part."

Patty swallowed hard. *I really hope you're right,* she thought. "Thanks," she said quietly.

"I'd better get out to my seat before someone steals it," Madame said. She gave Patty a quick hug. "Remember everything I told you, Patty. And let the beauty of the music be your guide."

When Madame had left, Patty stood in the silent room with her eyes closed and took a long, deep breath.

"Patty, it's time to go backstage!" Patty looked up and saw Kerry's excited face peering in the door. "Are you ready?"

Patty glanced up at the clock and her stomach did a little leap. "I hope so," she said. She followed

Kerry and the other girls down the hall to the back-stage door.

As Patty waited to make her entrance, she snuck a peek out at the crowd. The auditorium was packed. Her parents and Jana were in the front row, near Madame Baril. She even saw a big group of kids from school.

Suddenly, the orchestra began playing. It was time. Patty smoothed the skirt of her tutu one last time, her palms damp against the crinkly lace. Her knees were shaking, but she willed them to stop. Then she leaped out onto the stage.

Patty held her final *arabesque* as long as she could, trying to extend the drama of the scene. Then she lowered her leg, and dropped down in a small curtsy to indicate that the last scene had ended. She couldn't believe it was over. She felt as if she had only been on stage for two minutes.

For a second, nothing happened. Instead of applause, Patty heard only her heartbeat, pounding from the exertion of the performance. Beside her, one of the other girls' shoes squeaked slightly on the wood floor.

Oh, no, Patty thought. *I've blown it.*

Then, she heard a ripple of applause. It grew louder and louder, and soon the entire crowd was applauding wildly. Patty had never heard so much noise at one of her performances.

Slowly, she lifted her head. She saw her parents and sister grinning from ear to ear, standing up in front of their seats. Then she saw Madame Baril stand up, too, clapping her hands as hard as she could. As Patty straightened up to take a bow with the other girls, she saw that everyone was on their feet.

"It's a standing ovation," Kerry whispered excitedly, taking Patty's hand for their group bow.

Patty felt a tear trickle down her cheek. Next to her, Kerry squeezed her hand.

Patty knew she would never have another night like this, no matter how many more performances she gave.

"Honey, these are for you." Patty's father held out a huge bouquet of flowers.

"Thanks, Dad." Patty took the flowers, set them down on the chair backstage, and gave her father a hug.

"We're so proud of you," Mrs. Gilbert said. She hugged Patty too.

Next Jana wrapped her arms around Patty. "Are you doing OK?" Jana whispered.

Patty smiled and nodded, trying not to cry. She couldn't remember ever feeling so happy and so sad at once.

"You were great, Patty," Elizabeth said, handing her a pink rose. Jessica, Mandy, Mary, Grace, and Maria clustered around to congratulate her.

A moment later Patty saw Madame Baril walking toward her.

"Here is my ballerina," Madame said, giving her a hug. "You were wonderful, Patty. I've never seen you dance more beautifully."

"Thank you," Patty said.

Madame gestured her aside. "Can I speak with you privately for a moment?"

Patty felt her stomach tighten. Those were the words that had begun her troubles. What now?

"There is another story I haven't told you," Madame began. "You see, I already taught one girl who developed scoliosis. She was a beautiful dancer, just as you are. She came to class and danced when she could. But that wasn't enough for a girl of her talent."

Patty nodded, holding her breath. Was Madame going to tell her she might as well not bother dancing at all anymore?

"That is why I asked her to become my assistant teacher," Madame continued. "And that is what I wish to ask you."

Patty stared at her in relief and surprise.

"Would you like to be my assistant?"

Patty finally found her voice. "I–I would love that!"

"Good." Madame Baril looked at her seriously. "It will be difficult, Patty. You'll have to sit by and watch, knowing you won't be able to win the lead roles for a while. But you can continue your development while helping me teach. And as soon as your brace is off, you can bet that I will get you back in performances."

Patty nodded, swallowing past the lump in her throat.

"You have something special, Patty. No one can take that away from you."

"One last thing before we go," Mr. Gilbert said, as Patty gathered her things. "A photo of our ballet star on the stage."

"OK," Patty said, following her father into the now-deserted auditorium.

"Now, this is for posterity, so let's make it good," her father directed from the front of the stage. "I know this is a night we're going to want to remember."

Patty stood in the middle of the big empty stage, considering how she'd like to look back on this performance.

"OK, ready?" her father called.

Suddenly Patty broke her pose. "Wait a second," she called, running off stage. "I'll be right back."

She made her way through the hallway and down to the locker room, where she found Kerry packing up her dance bag.

"Hey, Kerry, will you come up to the stage for a second?" Patty asked.

"Sure, how come?" Kerry asked, heaving her bag over her shoulder.

"I wanted a picture of the two of us. You know, for when we're famous someday," Patty said with a grin.

"OK, are you guys ready? Say cheese!" Mr. Gilbert yelled as Patty pulled Kerry in front of the camera.

Just before the picture was snapped, Patty reached over and put her arm around Kerry's shoulders.

That was the way she wanted to remember this night.

Thirteen

◇

"How's it going so far?" Aaron Dallas asked Jessica, surveying the gym.

"Horribly," Jessica told him, dancing slowly from side to side. It was a few minutes past ten o'clock, and the marathon had officially started. The gym floor was full of people dancing—only it wasn't full enough.

"Come on, it's not that bad," Mandy said, dancing next to her. "We got all the decorations up, people are coming with food, the music's great—"

"Yeah, and Hollywood Jones isn't here," Jessica grumbled. "I'll bet he's at Big Mesa watching people jump around with their legs tied together."

"He's probably just late," Aaron said. "Big stars are always fashionably late, right?" He shuffled next to Jessica and she couldn't help giggling. Somehow it was hard to get in the right mood for a dance at ten in the morning.

"How many people are here?" Ellen asked. "Do we have enough?"

Jessica nodded. "As long as everyone keeps dancing. We have about a hundred here, and there have to be ninety to break the record. So only ten people can drop out."

"Oh, really? Maybe I'll just head over to the doughnut table—" Aaron began.

Jessica glared at him. "Aaron!"

"Only kidding!" Aaron held up his hands. "I'm going to go say hi to Ken. Catch you later."

Jessica looked around at the crowd. Winston Egbert was clowning around with Grace Oliver and Maria Slater. Bruce Patman was surrounded by Tamara Chase, Kimberly Haver, Betsy Gordon, and a few other seventh-grade girls. They seemed to be talking more than dancing. Every so often Bruce would sway a little bit. Jessica hoped that qualified as dancing.

Suddenly Mandy elbowed Jessica in the side. "Don't look now, but here comes Hollywood Jones," Mandy said with a big smile.

Jessica straightened her shirt and ran a hand over her hair. "OK, everybody, pretend you're having a great time," she said as Hollywood Jones made his way over to them. He looked as cool and handsome as ever.

"Looks like you're off to a great start," Hollywood called to the group. "Jim, get a few shots of them, will you?" he told the cameraman.

Jessica put on her biggest, most photogenic smile. "Only ten and a half hours to go," she called cheerfully as the camera focused on her.

Beside her, Hollywood was surveying the gym. He cleared his throat. "Excuse me, but you don't have two hundred people here, do you?"

Jessica laughed nervously. "Well, uh, maybe not right this *second*," she said, trying to sound casual. "But, you know, people are on breaks and stuff."

Hollywood looked at his watch. "Breaks? But you just started."

"Oh, well, um, we had to stagger the breaks, so there'd always be lots of people dancing," Jessica said.

Hollywood gave her a suspicious look. He glanced around the dance floor, and for a second Jessica thought she actually saw him counting. She threw Mandy a panicked look.

"So," she interrupted him. "How about a tour of our school?"

Hollywood looked at her as if she were crazy. "Don't you need to keep dancing?"

"Well, it's almost time for my break," Jessica said.

"No, that's OK. We have to get over to Big Mesa anyway," Hollywood said. "We'll be back later. When we do, I hope to see that huge crowd you promised, OK?'' He winked at Jessica and gave her a big smile.

It was kind of a phony smile, actually, Jessica decided. For once, she didn't feel like swooning. She didn't see why he had to act like such a jerk. So what if they didn't have exactly two hundred people? They had a hundred, which was more than enough to break the dumb record.

"He sounded kind of mad," Janet observed when Hollywood was gone. "Do you think he'll really come back?"

"He has to," Jessica said firmly. "He promised."

"Maybe we should try to get some more people," Mandy said. "I mean, a hundred and fifty-eight people did sign up. What if we called and reminded them that they're supposed to be here?"

"Do you have fifty-eight quarters?" Jessica asked, frowning.

"Well, what do *you* think we should do?" Mandy retorted.

"I don't know, but if Hollywood Jones doesn't let us be on his stupid show, I'll never forgive him," Jessica declared.

"I'm sorry, Jessica, I just don't feel very good," Lloyd Benson said.

"But it's only four o'clock. Can't you dance for

one more hour?" Jessica asked. "Sixty lousy minutes?"

"I feel like I'm going to keel over any second," Lloyd said. "I must be getting the flu or something. Anyway, good luck." He turned and walked toward the door.

"I can't believe it," Mandy moaned. "That's the fourth person who's dropped out already."

"At this rate the gym will be practically empty by the end of the marathon," Jessica said. "What's wrong with these people? Don't they care about being on TV?"

"Well, I don't know about the others," Lila commented. "But I think Lloyd really was sick. He looked a little green around the gills to me."

"We've got to make sure everyone who's left keeps dancing," Jessica said grimly. "I don't care if they suddenly come down with pneumonia."

Just then Hollywood walked in. Jessica mustered her brightest smile, even though she was feeling exhausted. Hollywood stopped to chat with a few of the dancers before coming over to her. "So, how's it going, organizers?" he asked Mandy and Jessica.

"Great!" Mandy said enthusiastically. She started dancing even faster.

"Would you like a brownie?" Jessica said, grabbing one from the refreshment table.

Hollywood stared at it for a moment and wrinkled his nose. "Uh, no thanks." He peered around the gym. "I still only count about a hundred kids. When you talked to my assistant, you said you had two hundred people."

"Your assistant?" Lila asked. "I thought she talked to you."

Hollywood laughed. "Me? I doubt that. I don't take calls from just anyone. My assistant handles all the arrangements." Jessica felt like sinking into the floor. Hollywood may be gorgeous, Jessica decided, but he wasn't exactly the nicest person she had ever met.

"Getting back to my point, where are those other ninety-eight people you promised?" Hollywood asked.

"Well, we just lost one person because he was sick," Jessica said. She pretended to concentrate on her dancing for a minute. "Actually, there's a big flu epidemic going around school."

"Oh yeah? Everyone looked fine yesterday when we did your interview," Hollywood said.

"It's one of those flus that comes on really fast," Jessica said. "Once you get it, you can't move or anything. We probably had two hundred around noon, but . . . well, you know. The epidemic."

"I had it at the beginning of the week," Mandy said. She coughed. "Actually, I still don't feel too good."

Jessica smiled at her gratefully.

"We're still going to break the record," Lila

said. "I mean, we have enough people and everything."

"Oh, I don't care about the record. I'm just afraid that this isn't going to look very impressive on TV." Hollywood surveyed the gym again. "Boy, you should have seen the crowd at Big Mesa. What a party."

Jessica couldn't help rolling her eyes at Mandy.

"In fact," Hollywood went on, "we've probably got enough footage from that to fill the whole episode."

Jessica almost dropped the brownie she was holding. "Are you saying we might not be on the show?"

"Well, let's just say I'll check back here later. See how things look."

Jessica glared at his back as he walked over to the refreshment table. She had just about had it with Hollywood Jones. But after all her hard work, she was going to get on his stupid show if it was the last thing she did.

"I just checked with Jessica's dad, and there are only fourteen official minutes left until we break the record," Mandy told everyone excitedly.

Jessica glanced up at the clock on the gym wall. It was a little after nine o'clock in the evening. She looked over and saw Hollywood in the corner with his makeup man, intently examining his hair in the mirror. *Ugh*, she thought.

But just then she had a great idea.

"OK, everybody," she yelled. "We're almost there. Just fourteen minutes to go, so let's make it a big finale!"

"Jessica, what are you talking about? Everybody is totally sick of this," Lila whined.

Jessica ignored her. "Hey, Dad, could you please put on a Johnny Buck tape?" she called. "And crank it up!"

Everyone was staring at her as though she'd lost her mind.

"Everybody line up behind me," Jessica yelled.

Out of the corner of her eye she saw Patty Gilbert smile at her and dance over. "I think I know what you're getting at," she said, standing behind Jessica and putting her hands on Jessica's hips. Kerry and Mandy hurried over and lined up behind Patty.

"Let's go," Jessica cried.

Suddenly Johnny Buck's voice came booming across the dance floor and the girls took off in a line. Patty, Kerry and Mandy copied Jessica's moves perfectly. Elizabeth, Amy, and Maria started laughing and joined the line. "Come on," Maria cried, gesturing to Sophia Rizzo and Patrick Morris. They looked at each other, shrugged, and joined in. Pretty soon, all ninety-six people were dancing around the room in a long line like a giant centipede.

Jessica glanced over her shoulder happily. For

the first time all day, everybody was laughing and having a great time. *Let's hope this works*, she said to herself as she led the line past Hollywood Jones. She noticed he hadn't even looked up from his mirror.

"Hollywood, come on!" Jessica yelled.

Hollywood looked up for a moment and shook his head. "No, thanks."

"Oh, come on," Jessica urged him. She gave him her biggest smile. "Think how *great* it'll look on your show."

That was all it took. Hollywood set his cup of water and his notebook on the floor and ran up to the very front of the line, ahead of Jessica. "Follow me, everybody!" he cried.

"Figures," Jessica muttered to his back as the cameraman walked in front of them, pointing the camera directly at Hollywood.

A few minutes later, the music suddenly stopped, and Mr. Wakefield yelled, "You did it! You did it! Time!" He pointed to the big clock behind the basketball hoop.

"We did it!" Jessica cried.

"Yahoo!" Mandy screamed.

Everyone crowded around them, and Hollywood Jones was caught in a group hug. The cameraman moved closer for a clearer picture. "Easy!" Hollywood cried. "I can't breathe!"

Jessica grinned. That was one shot she knew she'd see on TV—Hollywood Jones, the man with the biggest ego on the planet, being mobbed by fans.

"I can't believe Hollywood Jones had the nerve to have his assistant call me," Jessica said on the following Wednesday afternoon. "Pretty typical, I guess."

"Well, his assistant's the one who *knows* you, after all," Lila said with a smirk.

The Unicorns, Elizabeth, Kerry, Patty, Amy, Maria, Melissa McCormick, and Julie Porter were all sitting in the Wakefields' living room waiting for *You'll Never Believe This!* to come on.

"The only person in the world who's more obnoxious than Hollywood Jones is my new neighbor, Veronica Brooks," Lila was complaining to Ellen. "I ran into her yesterday when I was riding my bike, and she acted as if she'd never even met me before. Like I don't see her every day in math class!"

"I guess your singing turned her off," Jessica said.

"Wait—here it is!" Amy cried.

Hollywood Jones was smiling into the camera. "Hello, everyone, and welcome to—"

The audience excitedly screamed the name of the show.

"Oh, just get on with it already," Jessica grumbled.

"He's such a phony," Janet complained.

"Yeah, but he's still gorgeous," Mandy said.

Patty laughed and poked Mandy in the back. Mandy turned around and smiled. "I can't help it—he is!"

Hollywood Jones went over to his director's chair. "We have a really hot show for you today, folks. We'll be traveling to Sweet Valley to show you—hey, why don't we just show you now? Get ready, folks—this is wild!"

The screen behind Hollywood lit up, and there was his face again, taking up practically the whole screen. But suddenly the camera moved away and Patty saw her own face. The camera moved farther back, and she saw herself dancing and laughing, surrounded by Jessica, Elizabeth, Mandy, Kerry, Mary, and all of her other new friends as they hopped around the room behind Hollywood.

"And get this, folks," Hollywood Jones announced. "They danced like this for more than *eleven* hours. Can you believe it?"

"All right, Patty!" Mandy yelled.

"You look great," Kerry said. "Like you're really having fun!"

"I was," Patty said, smiling.

The following Friday afternoon, Elizabeth couldn't wait to get out of science class, her last class of the day. She and Amy were going on a bike ride to the beach right after school.

"Before I let you go, I'd like to return your tests from yesterday," Mr. Seigel said. "For the most part, they were pretty good." He walked around the classroom, distributing the corrected tests.

"Nice job, Elizabeth," Mr. Seigel said as he placed her test on her desk. Elizabeth glanced at it. She'd gotten two questions wrong.

When she looked up, she was surprised to see Veronica Brooks turned around in her chair, staring at her. "What did you get?" Veronica asked.

Elizabeth looked down at her paper. "A ninety-four," she said. "Why?"

Veronica frowned. "I only got a ninety-two. But I think he graded me wrong on one of the questions."

"You can always ask him to grade it again," Elizabeth said. She didn't understand why anyone would be upset about getting a ninety-two.

"I can tell he only did it because I'm new here," Veronica said angrily. "But just watch—I'm going to do better than you on our next test." Then she turned back around and faced the blackboard, where Mr. Seigel was writing down their homework assignment.

Elizabeth didn't know what to think about her new classmate. Why did Veronica care how Elizabeth did?

What does Veronica Brooks have against Elizabeth? Find out in Sweet Valley Twins and Friends #66, THE GREAT BOYFRIEND SWITCH.

SWEET VALLEY TWINS™

☐	15681-0	TEAMWORK #27	$2.75
☐	15688-8	APRIL FOOL! #28	$3.25
☐	15695-0	JESSICA AND THE BRAT ATTACK #29	$2.99
☐	15715-9	PRINCESS ELIZABETH #30	$2.99
☐	15727-2	JESSICA'S BAD IDEA #31	$3.25
☐	15747-7	JESSICA ON STAGE #32	$2.99
☐	15753-1	ELIZABETH'S NEW HERO #33	$2.99
☐	15766-3	JESSICA, THE ROCK STAR #34	$3.25
☐	15772-8	AMY'S PEN PAL #35	$2.99
☐	15778-7	MARY IS MISSING #36	$3.25
☐	15779-5	THE WAR BETWEEN THE TWINS #37	$3.25
☐	15789-2	LOIS STRIKES BACK #38	$2.99
☐	15798-1	JESSICA AND THE MONEY MIX-UP #39	$3.25
☐	15806-6	DANNY MEANS TROUBLE #40	$3.25
☐	15810-4	THE TWINS GET CAUGHT #41	$3.25
☐	15824-4	JESSICA'S SECRET #42	$2.99
☐	15835-X	ELIZABETH'S FIRST KISS #43	$2.99
☐	15837-6	AMY MOVES IN #44	$3.25
☐	15843-0	LUCY TAKES THE REINS #45	$3.25
☐	15849-X	MADEMOISELLE JESSICA #46	$3.25
☐	15869-4	JESSICA'S NEW LOOK #47	$3.25
☐	15880-5	MANDY MILLER FIGHTS BACK #48	$3.25
☐	15899-6	THE TWINS' LITTLE SISTER #49	$2.99
☐	15911-9	JESSICA AND THE SECRET STAR #50	$3.25

Bantam Books, Dept. SVT5, 2451 S. Wolf Road, Des Plaines, IL 60018

Please send me the items I have checked above. I am enclosing $_____.
(please add $2.50 to cover postage and handling). Send check or money
order, no cash or C.O.D.s please.

Mr/Ms _____

Address _____

City/State _____ Zip _____

SVT5-12/92

Please allow four to six weeks for delivery.
Prices and availability subject to change without notice.